THE SIGN OF THE TWISTED CANDLES

ANOTHER exciting mystery begins for the attractive young detective when her friends Bess and George ask her to investigate a rumor that their wealthy great-granduncle, Asa Sidney, is virtually a prisoner in his own mansion. But solving the mystery and befriending Carol Wipple, the sixteen-year-old foster daughter of the caretakers of the old mansion, nearly costs Nancy the friendship of Bess and George. It takes all of Nancy's sleuthing ability as well as diplomacy to save it.

At the same time, Nancy braves one danger after another to bring to justice the swindlers who are stealing Asa Sidney's fortune. With only the sign of the twisted candles to guide her, Nancy uncovers hidden treasure and an amazing letter that ends a family feud and brings unexpected happiness to Carol.

Mr. Drew reached out to rescue Nancy

The Sign
of the
Twisted Candles

BY CAROLYN KEENE

PUBLISHERS   *Grosset & Dunlap*   NEW YORK

Contents

The Sign
of the
Twisted Candles

CHAPTER I

The Tower Room

"Oh, Nancy, this is like a hurricane! We'll be blown off the road!" cried Bess Marvin.

"We'd better try to go on," Nancy Drew told the worried girl beside her in the convertible.

"Yes," said George Fayne, the other girl with them. "A tree might fall on us. I'll bet this wind is a hundred miles an hour!"

Bess, her cousin, shuddered. "No mystery is worth our taking this chance."

The three friends were headed for a secluded inn called The Sign of the Twisted Candles. The Marvin family and the Faynes were related to a very old man who lived there. Rumors had recently come from neighbors of theirs who had overheard a conversation at the inn that he was virtually a prisoner in the tower of the old-fashioned mansion.

1

Bess and George had never been there and had asked attractive, titian-haired Nancy to drive out to investigate the rumors. If there was a mystery, it would be a challenge to Nancy, affectionately called by her friends "our detective." It had been agreed that the girls' mission to the inn would be kept secret from its occupants.

"It's our mothers' uncle we're going to see. His name is Asa Sidney," said George. "He owns the place, but turned over the management of it a few years ago to a couple named Jemitt."

Trees and bushes swayed in the wind, which had blown up suddenly and now shrieked like a siren. It slammed against the car with terrific force as dust and leaves swirled through the air.

"Oh!" Bess screamed suddenly. "Look!"

Not far ahead of the car a giant elm had started to topple. As Nancy jammed on her brakes, the tree fell with a thundering crash across the road.

The three girls sat stunned, but finally Bess said, "Now we'll have to turn around and go home."

"Don't be silly," said George. "I can see the inn just beyond the tree. We can walk there."

Nancy drove up to the tree, which might offer protection for the car against the storm's blast. She and her friends stepped out into the wind, which whipped their hair and stung their faces. With eyes almost closed, they locked arms, skirted the fallen tree, and set off for the inn.

Nancy jammed on her brakes

Progress was slow, but finally they came to the inn's spacious front lawn and curving driveway at the end of the road. Several cars were parked there. The building was a rambling structure in three sections. Its central portion was two stories high and had a flat-roofed tower room. Wings on either side were one story and also flat-roofed.

There was a dim glow of light from the ground-floor windows. In the arched casement of the tower a sturdy candlelight gleamed a welcome. Almost breathless, the three girls dashed up the broad front steps onto the wide porch just as it started to rain.

George glanced at the parked cars and remarked with a grin, "I wonder what their drivers will say when they see that fallen tree across the road."

"They'll be wild," Bess prophesied, and added, "I'm sure I look a fright." She ran her fingers through her tousled, blond hair.

George, a brunette with short hair, remarked, "Who wouldn't, when we've just barely escaped being blown into space!"

Nancy led the way to the door and opened it. The three girls found themselves in a long hall, lighted only by electric sconces on the walls. The candle bulbs in them were large and twisted.

To the left and right arched doorways opened into high-ceilinged rooms where tables, each with a similar candle, were set in rows. Half a dozen couples looked up curiously as the girls entered, then resumed eating.

From a doorway in the rear of the hall a woman wearing a black dress with a small, frilled white apron approached Nancy and her friends.

"Good afternoon," Nancy said. "We'd like to have some tea and cinnamon toast, and stay here until the storm dies down."

The woman, a gaunt, thin-lipped person past middle age, nodded her head.

"Just take any table," she replied.

"Is there a room where we can comb our hair?" Nancy asked.

The woman nodded. "Go to the head of the stairs. You'll see a powder room there."

The girls climbed the creaky staircase to the upper hall and opened the door marked *Ladies*. They washed their hands, then began to comb their hair. Suddenly they heard an angry masculine voice outside the door.

"Where do you think you're going with that?"

Nancy, alert to any clue in the mystery at the inn, turned to her friends, fingers to her lips. A girl's voice replied, but the three visitors had difficulty hearing what was said because of the roaring wind.

"He's one hundred today, so I thought you wouldn't mind—"

"It's too much!" shouted the man. "Take that tray back! There are three young ladies just in to be fed. Get downstairs and help. And be quick about it!"

"But on his hundredth birthday—" the girl protested.

"No back talk! I'll take something to the tower later."

Nancy and her friends were startled by the crash of glass on the first floor and assumed that the wind had blown in several panes. Quick footsteps indicated the man was running down the steps.

The door of the powder room creaked on its hinges and slowly opened inward. Hesitatingly a slender girl of about sixteen came into view. She seemed to be dazed and frightened. Was it from fear of the storm or of the man?

Like the woman who had greeted them, the girl wore a black dress with a frilled white apron. Clenched in her hands was a tray. A bouquet of flowers and several dishes of food were in imminent danger of sliding to the floor.

"Here, let me take that," Nancy said quickly.

"Oh! Who—?"

The girl gave a faint scream and swayed. Nancy seized the tray, thrust it into the hands of the amazed Bess, then put an arm about the girl's quivering form.

As Bess and George regarded the frightened girl with pity, Nancy led her to a couch and gently urged her to sit down.

"Just take it easy," she said. "I think the wind is dying down a little. Maybe there won't be any more trouble."

The girl sank down obediently. "No more trouble?" she muttered.

Then suddenly she leaped to her feet. "Oh, what am I thinking of?" she cried out. "I—I must go! At once! The twisted candles—"

"The twisted candles?" Nancy repeated.

"Yes, I should help him light them. It's getting dark."

Nancy, Bess, and George exchanged sideways glances, then Nancy asked, "He? The man who was in the hall?"

"Oh, no, the one who lives in the tower. He's a dear old man, but—" The girl stopped speaking and looked into space.

After a pause she went on, "I'll be right down to serve you." But she lingered as if wanting to tell something else.

When she remained silent, Nancy said, "I'm Nancy Drew. These are my friends Bess Marvin and George Fayne." On purpose she slurred the last names so the girl could not repeat them.

"I'm Carol Wipple," the waitress replied. "I—I must do what the Jemitts say. I can't stand here talking. I must get to work, or else—"

"Or else what?" Nancy asked. "In the excitement no one will miss you for a few minutes."

George spoke up. "If I were you, Carol, I'd take

the tray upstairs. The man in the tower has to eat."

"I'd like to, but I don't dare," Carol said, her eyes widening with fear. "I was forbidden."

Nancy saw a chance to do some sleuthing. Perhaps *she* could go to the tower. "But this tray of food—it'll go to waste," she said. "It's for Mr. —"

"Mr. Asa Sidney. He lives alone in the tower room. He's one hundred years old today."

Nancy smiled. "I should like to meet a man one hundred years old. And I certainly think he deserves a party on his birthday—a real celebration."

"Mr. Jemitt thinks it is too expensive a trayful," Carol said. "You see, Mr. Sidney lets my foster parents, Frank and Emma Jemitt, use this property in exchange for taking care of him. I don't know why I'm telling you girls all this."

"You're not to worry," Nancy said firmly. "I'll pay for the food on the tray, and I'll carry it up and serve it myself."

"Oh, would you do that?" Carol cried happily.

From somewhere downstairs a voice thundered, "Carol! Where are you?"

"Oh, I must go!" Carol said, and darted from the room.

"Nancy, you old dear," Bess said affectionately. "You're always putting yourself out to be kind to others."

"And you did a great bit of sleuthing," George

remarked. "I'd like to meet Asa Sidney, but Mr. Jemitt might become suspicious if we all barge in on him."

"That's right," said Bess. "Nancy, why don't you go alone?"

"Okay, but I'll try to work out something so you girls can come up too."

Bess and George said they would share the expense of Mr. Sidney's dinner, then went down to the dining room. Nancy climbed the stairs, carrying the tray. The stairway was unlighted, and the swaying tree branches made queer-shaped shadows on the walls. The door above was closed.

"A perfect setting for a spooky mystery," Nancy thought. "The biggest problem right now is how I'm going to knock on the door, with both hands balancing this tray!"

She reached the top of the stairway and stood in front of the heavy paneled door. A dim light showed beneath it, but no sound came from the other side.

"I'll just tap on the door with my foot," Nancy decided.

Leaning against the doorframe, she tapped with one heel. To her surprise the door swung silently open. Evidently the lock had not caught fast.

Nancy gazed into one of the strangest rooms she had ever seen. It was fully twenty feet square, and from all of its walls candles gleamed—candles by the dozen, all winking in the draft from the open door. Evidently Mr. Sidney had not waited for Carol to light them.

It was warm in the room, and the heavy air was pungently scented by burning tallow. In the great arched window directly in front of Nancy was the massive twisted candle whose light she had seen from outdoors.

From a low, broad chair before this window, the gaunt figure of a very old man arose. The candlelight showed his long, silver-white hair sweeping over stooped shoulders, and merging with the snowy beard that spread across his chest. Shaggy white eyebrows half concealed glowing eyes—strangely youthful eyes—that peered at Nancy from either side of a jutting, hawklike nose.

"Good evenng," she said. "I have brought your dinner."

The old man stretched out his bony, trembling arms. In a deep, husky voice that faltered as he spoke, Asa Sidney cried out:

"Jenny—my Jenny, you've come back to me!"

CHAPTER II

Trouble Ahead

NANCY looked at Asa Sidney with deep perplexity, wondering who Jenny was.

"I think you're mistaken," she said, smiling. "I'm Nancy Drew, and this is the first time I've ever been here. . . . Oh, how very odd!"

She set the tray down on a bench and gazed at a portrait over the fireplace. It was a fine oil painting of a titian-haired young woman who resembled Nancy. She realized that in the flickering candlelight she must look very much like the person in the portrait.

"I—I must have been dreaming," Asa Sidney murmured, dropping his arms and shaking his head. "Well, well," he continued, "that's all we old folks have left. If it were not for our dreams, we should be poor indeed."

Nancy was silent, not certain just what reply, if any, was expected from her.

"However," Asa Sidney went on, looking at her with a smile, "you were a very lovely vision as you entered the room. While drowsing, I seemed to see my dear wife step down from the picture up there. If I can't tell a very pretty and very much alive young woman from an old piece of canvas and paint, then I shall have to visit an oculist."

Nancy chuckled. "May I congratulate you on your hundredth birthday?" she said. "Carol fixed this tray for you."

Asa Sidney laughed a little bitterly. "Pardon me, my dear," he said, sitting down again. "I'm afraid I've become a lonely, cross old hermit. Carol is a good girl, a very thoughtful young person, to remember a date that means nothing to anybody else."

"Surely it is worth while to celebrate one's hundredth birthday," Nancy remarked. "Why, your name should be in the papers, and your picture, too."

"No, no," protested the old man. "That's all vanity and display. Why should I be honored for my existence? I haven't tried to live longer than anyone else. I've read interviews in the newspapers. The reporters always ask the centenarians how they managed to live so long. One old codger will say he got to be a hundred because he never ate meat, and another will say he attributes his old age to the fact that he never ate anything but meat!"

Asa Sidney gave a mirthless laugh. "The only reason I have lived to be a hundred is because I have not died!"

Nancy shuddered a little. Plainly Mr. Sidney was far from happy.

"You must have many visitors," Nancy suggested.

"No," the old man said sadly, "not a soul ever comes to see me."

Nancy knew this was not true. She asked, "Are you sure?"

"Of course. The Jemitts have told me."

The young detective decided not to pursue the subject. It might upset the old man to learn that Bess and George's relatives had been told Asa Sidney would see no one.

She said abruptly, *"I'd* like to celebrate your birthday. Two darling friends of mine are downstairs. May we have tea up here with you as a sort of birthday party? Perhaps Carol will join us."

Mr. Sidney looked startled. "What did you say your name is?"

"Nancy Drew. My father is Carson Drew, the attorney."

"An attorney, eh?" Asa Sidney paused. "Well, Nancy, bring up your young friends. Tell Jemitt to send us the best food in the inn, and say I will pay what exceeds my usual portion."

"You are very kind, Mr. Sidney," said Nancy, "but it is not necessary to do that."

The old man's conversation strengthened Nancy's growing suspicion that the Jemitts, for reasons of their own, wanted to keep the old man a virtual prisoner. She sped down the stairs and joined George and Bess.

"There you are at last!" Bess cried. "I've almost died sitting here being polite, while all the time this was teasing me."

"This" proved to be a plateful of golden cinnamon toast from which Bess lifted the cover.

"Wait a minute!" Nancy cried.

"Wait a minute? Oh, Nancy!" Bess protested.

In a whisper the young detective told of her visit to the tower. Her friends' eyes opened wide in surprise at what she had learned.

"We're going to have dinner up there," Nancy announced. "I'll call Hannah, and she can phone your parents."

She rang a little bell on the table, and Carol came to answer.

"Carol," said Nancy, "all of us are going to have a birthday dinner with Mr. Sidney. He invited us."

"Oh!" the young waitress exclaimed. "I'm afraid—"

As Nancy took hold of Carol's hand, she wondered, "Does Jemitt have *everybody* intimidated?" Aloud she said, "Please tell Mr. Jemitt to come here."

Jemitt was a tall, rather heavy-set man, slightly bald. "Yes, miss?" the manager asked, his voice purring as he bowed to Nancy.

"We've decided to have a more substantial meal," Nancy said. "Of course we'll pay for the tea and toast."

Jemitt bowed more deeply.

"We'll have jellied consommé, sliced breast of chicken, hearts of lettuce with Roquefort dressing, nut bread, ice cream, chocolate layer cake, and fruit punch," Nancy said, mentioning the items that had been on Carol's tray for Mr. Sidney.

"That sounds good to me," murmured Bess, and George nodded in agreement.

The man bowed and replied, "I shall hurry your orders, miss."

"One thing more," Nancy said. "We want this meal served in the tower room with Mr. Sidney, and I should like very much to have you give permission for Carol to join us."

The suave, sleek Jemitt bristled. "What is the meaning of this? What do you know of the tower room? I—why—who are you?"

"It doesn't matter." Nancy smiled. "We wish to celebrate Mr. Sidney's birthday and he would like us to eat with him. We'll pay for our dinner and also for the tray Carol fixed for him."

Nancy's outspoken manner seemed to intimidate the man. He bowed again and left the room.

George grinned. "Nancy, you sure took him by surprise."

Nancy smiled. "Now I'll phone Hannah, then take you girls up and introduce you to Mr. Sidney."

The line was busy, however, so she led her friends toward the stairs.

Carol came toward them. "How did you ever persuade Mr. Jemitt to let me join you?" she whispered. "He's furious, but he doesn't dare offend a patron or lose a big order."

"I'm glad he thinks I'm a worthwhile customer," Nancy answered with a wink.

As she climbed to the tower, Nancy was thoughtful. Carol was evidently browbeaten and unhappy. Was this part of the mystery at the old inn? Yet there seemed to be a bond between the thin, timid girl and Asa Sidney—a bond which the Jemitts did not approve.

Nancy had arrived at no conclusion when the girls reached the door of the tower room and knocked. Bess and George gave a little start when they saw the ghostly room and its elderly occupant.

"I'm afraid you'll find this strange tower of mine scarcely prepared for your delightful visit," Mr. Sidney said with quaint courtesy. "However, you are most welcome."

Bess and George gazed at the twisted candles

that gleamed everywhere. Along one side stood a wide couch which evidently served the recluse as a bed. On the opposite wall were framed patent grants for things he had invented.

One entire side of the room was occupied by an open charcoal furnace and a worktable. On the table stood pots, pans, dye vats, bars of tallow and beeswax, and rows of pewter candle molds. Nancy introduced her friends merely as Bess and George, and was glad when Mr. Sidney did not ask for their last names.

The cousins were silent, obviously awed by the strange surroundings and the remarkable spectacle the old man made as he moved about the room. The candlelight gave an aura of glowing silver to his mass of hair. He kept scoffing at himself for being slow and clumsy.

"Oh, I'm forgetting my phone call!" Nancy exclaimed. "The line was busy when I tried it before." She had noted there was no phone in the tower. Therefore Mr. Sidney did not have this means of communicating with the outside world.

As Nancy went down the stairway, now dimly lighted with wall candles, she heard someone ascending. It was Jemitt, grumbling under his breath and carrying a large covered tray. A few steps behind came Carol, similarly burdened.

"Ah, miss, I'll be ready for you in a moment," Jemitt said pleasantly.

"I'm going down to phone," Nancy explained.

She closed herself into the booth. In a moment Hannah Gruen, the warmhearted, efficient house-keeper of the Drew household, answered.

"Hello. This is Nancy."

"Thank goodness you called," Hannah said. "I was getting worried. Did you find the place?"

"Oh, yes, it's very quaint. I'll tell you about it when I get home. Bess and George and I are having dinner here. Will you please call their parents for them."

"Glad to. But I want to know, did you speak to their relative?"

"Yes. I must go now."

"Tell me first, what's his name?"

"Sidney—Asa Sidney. It's his birth—"

"Asa Sidney!" Hannah cried out. "Oh, Nancy, now you're in for trouble!"

Click!

The line suddenly went dead, and although Nancy tried for five minutes to have the connection restored, she was unsuccessful. Evidently the wind had blown down some wires.

Nancy climbed the stairs, more puzzled than ever. How could old Asa Sidney make trouble for her?

CHAPTER III

The Feud

"COME and sit down, my dear! The celebration has already begun," old Mr. Sidney greeted Nancy as she re-entered the tower room.

"I'm sorry to have been so long," Nancy remarked as she sat down in the rocking chair.

"Jemitt has made some excellent fruit punch," he told her.

"Then I propose a toast to you, Mr. Sidney," Nancy said, lifting her glass high. "Happy Birthday!"

The four girls rose to their feet and sang the familiar birthday song. Tears of happiness glistened in the eyes of the old man, and even his beard could not conceal the pleased smile that spread over his face.

"Thank you, thank you," he murmured.

The candlelight sparkled on the silver and china, and Bess and George relaxed in the gaiety of the birthday party. Even Carol's timidity seemed to vanish.

Nancy, Bess, and George each told a humorous story, and Mr. Sidney laughed in delight. Finally Nancy asked him about candle making.

"It began in England," the old man replied as he finished his cake. "I was born in Liverpool-on-Tyne. When I was still a boy I went to work for a chandler—a man who makes candles."

"Was the work hard?" Bess asked.

"For the first year I carried wood and stoked the fires which melted the tallow," Mr. Sidney said. "It was hot work and the hours were long. Then I was promoted to stirring and skimming the hot grease. Under an arrangement with my parents, I was to live with my employer until I was eighteen. At that time I was to receive a new suit of clothes, some money, and a certificate to prove I was a journeyman chandler.

"It's not boasting to say that I learned quickly, and when I was fifteen I developed my first invention. I invented a candle that was pierced lengthwise by four holes, down which the melted tallow ran, instead of spilling over the candlestick. In this way it was saved, to be burned when the candle grew shorter. My employer made a good profit on that. I received nothing."

George said sympathetically, "How unjust!"

"It was, so I decided to run away. I had only the clothes I wore and no money, but I was determined to get to America," Mr. Sidney explained. "I offered to work my way across the ocean, and the captain of a freighter agreed to give me passage in exchange for labor as a helper in the galley.

"The ship ran into terrible storms and it took months to get to New York. Our drinking water ran low. I can tell you we were mighty glad to reach America and drop anchor.

"I soon found steady work making candles," Asa Sidney went on. "When I had a little money laid aside I opened my own shop, married, and had three children.

"Evenings I experimented with improvements on candles and—and I guess I neglected my children and my wife."

The white head bowed and a tremor ran through the old man's body. The girls remained respectfully silent.

"Eventually I invented the twisted candle which brought me fame and fortune."

At the phrase "fame and fortune" Nancy said to herself, "So this man, despite his surroundings, is no doubt wealthy." Her eyes roved around the room. A small ornate wooden chest under a low table caught her attention. Carved on the top were several twisted candles. There was a nameplate: *Private property of Asa Sidney.*

At the moment the old man was saying, "But fame and fortune did not help solve my problem. My little girl died and my wife and boys left me here alone. I never heard from them again. But years later I learned all of them had died. The boys had never married, so I have no descendants. I had a brother, though, who also came to America, but he has passed away."

"I'm terribly sorry," said Nancy, and Bess and George expressed their sympathy.

"Men should be content," Mr. Sidney said. "If they let success make them greedy, they lose the happiness money can't buy."

"But surely," Bess spoke up, "a successful man owes it to the world to use his talents for the general good."

"It was pride that urged me on, not a desire to better the world," the old man said.

Mr. Sidney's grief was so apparent that Nancy rose from her chair and put a hand on his quivering shoulder. "I'm sorry if we have revived sorrowful memories. Please don't be so sad."

"Sad? I'm doomed to be the saddest mortal on earth. Instead of a pleasant home, with my relatives coming to see me, I have lived to watch a feud. There is greed where there should be affection, and envy where there should be love!"

Nancy glanced at Bess and George, who shrugged. Apparently they had never been told about the feud.

Asa Sidney sat up straight and looked about him. "You must pardon me, my dears, for inflicting a half century of sorrow upon you. This is no

way to repay your kindness. Is there any fruit
punch left? Let us drink to the new world of elec-
tronics, spaceships, and trips to the moon—but always soft candlelight. Salute!"

All drained their glasses of fruit punch, Bess
looking wistfully at the maraschino cherry which
obstinately remained in the bottom of her glass.

Nancy saw that the old man was tiring and said
they must go. As she rose from her chair, they all
heard a bloodcurdling shriek from outdoors.
Nancy rushed to the window and looked down.
She could see no one, but in a moment Jemitt
rushed from the inn and gazed about. Apparently
he was puzzled too.

"I must go," Carol said quickly and hurried
downstairs.

The other girls said good night to Mr. Sidney
and followed. By the time they reached the first
floor, Jemitt was coming back inside.

"What happened?" Nancy asked.

"Search me," he replied. "Some crazy woman
just trying out her lungs, I guess. Did you enjoy
your dinner?"

"It was delicious. How much do I owe you?"

The manager named an amount and Nancy
paid the bill.

As the girls went to the front porch, Carol came
from the garden, saying she had not seen the
woman who screamed. "I hope she wasn't in-
jured."

Nancy was suspicious about the whole episode. Had Jemitt been eavesdropping at the tower room door, afraid Asa Sidney might say something to his visitors which would make them feel he was being mistreated? To get the girls away, had he ordered some woman, probably Mrs. Jemitt, to scream? If so, the ruse had worked!

Nancy did not express her thoughts aloud. Instead, she gave Carol a quick kiss and said, "Remember, my dad is a lawyer. If he or I can be of service to you, please let me know."

"I hope to see you again and often," Carol answered shyly, "even though I can't imagine myself needing legal advice."

Nancy, Bess, and George walked along the driveway to the road and set off for the convertible. The wind had died down but had left trees uprooted and branches snapped off.

They found Nancy's car undamaged and climbed in. She turned on the headlights and had just backed around when a car roared up the road and stopped short at the fallen tree. The driver almost scraped the fender of Nancy's car. He leaned out and asked curtly why she was blocking the road.

"Great-Uncle Peter!" George exclaimed. "Hello, Uncle Pete!"

"Who—what—George! And Bess, too? Yes, it is. What are you girls doing here?"

The man leaped from his car and strode toward

them, his face plainly showing annoyed surprise.

"We haven't seen you in a couple of years," Bess called, trying to force a cheery note into her voice.

Nancy watched the little drama with wonder. She had never heard of Great-Uncle Peter.

"You haven't answered my question. Why are you two here?" the man demanded.

"We were caught in the storm and stopped at The Sign of the Twisted Candles," George replied. "This is our friend, Nancy Drew. Our Great-Uncle, Nancy. Mr. Peter Boonton."

Peter Boonton, a tall, thin man about sixty, nodded acknowledgment of the introduction.

"Well, run along now," he admonished his nieces. "It is late for you girls to be so far from home." He turned on his heel and started toward the inn on foot.

"Whew!" George exclaimed. "What a greeting! Nancy, the plot thickens. Great-Uncle Peter must have come to see Asa Sidney. Well, let's go!"

Before Nancy could start, another car whizzed up the road and screeched to a halt.

"This place has become very popular all of a sudden," Bess remarked.

Since the newcomer was blocking the road, Nancy tapped her horn. Instead of moving, the driver sat staring at Peter Boonton's car. He called to Nancy, "Say, miss, do you know whose car that is? It looks like Pete Boonton's."

He stepped to the ground. The man appeared to be about the same age as Bess and George's great-uncle, but was heavier set.

"Yes, that's Pete's car all right," he declared emphatically. "See here, you aren't waiting for him by any chance, are you?"

"Certainly not," Nancy answered, gripping Bess's arm as a signal for silence. "We're just leaving, as a matter of fact."

"Don't let me keep you, then," the stranger said, leaning an elbow on Nancy's car. "Now that the owner of this place has hit the century mark, I suppose every relative of his or his wife is looking forward to a piece of his estate. They're worrying more about his money than his health, you can bet!" The man laughed loudly.

Here was added light on Asa Sidney's odd affairs, Nancy thought. She hoped the stranger would continue his musings.

"Yes sir! Two generations of bickering, and now—him! Well, Peter Boonton can't put anything over on me," the man muttered. "He's not a blood relative. There'll be a hot scene in the tower room tonight or I'm not Jacob Sidney!"

Bess and George gasped but said nothing. Nancy asked, "You are related to Asa Sidney?"

"Yes, my father was his brother. How do you know Asa?" he said, thrusting his face into Nancy's car. "Say, who are you?"

"Oh, I just met Mr. Sidney this evening,"

Nancy replied nonchalantly. "When I heard it was his hundredth birthday, I arranged a little party for him. Carol helped get it ready and ate with us."

"Carol! Humph! Asa thinks more of that girl than of his own flesh and blood."

"He seems to be very lonely," Nancy remarked pointedly. "He said so himself."

"Oh, he did, did he? And whom has he to blame for that?" Jacob Sidney shouted. "Cutting himself off from everybody and living in an attic making twisted candles all the time. He's crazy, that's what he is.

"You can bet that I'm not crazy enough to let Pete Boonton fill the old man with gossip," he added, shaking his fist at the house. "The Sidneys didn't inherit any weakness in the head, and a Boonton never got the best of 'em yet!"

With that, the man dashed off to the inn.

CHAPTER IV

A Strange Story

As Nancy headed the car for River Heights, Bess and George began to talk excitedly.

"I wonder what the feud is about," said Bess. "It must be pretty bad."

George nodded and Nancy told them about Hannah Gruen's remark, "Now you're in for trouble." The cousins could not figure out what she had meant, but said they would ask their parents.

"We'll let you know, Nancy, what they say," Bess promised.

Heavy storm damage to trees and flooding along the roads made driving hazardous and it was late before Nancy reached her own home. Mr. Drew heard her pull into the garage and opened the kitchen door.

"Hi, Dad!" Nancy cried, kissing him.

"Hello, Nancy! How's the junior partner of Drew and Drew, Incorporated?" The tall, handsome lawyer laughed.

"Full of mystery," she replied. "Wait'll you hear what happened. Hi, Hannah!" she said to the sweet, motherly-looking housekeeper who had just finished putting away the dinner dishes. She had helped rear Nancy since she was three, when Mrs. Drew had died.

Nancy said, "Let's all go into the living room and exchange stories. Dad, build a nice cozy fire, will you? It's chilly."

Soon there was a roaring blaze in the fireplace and the three sat down. Hannah Gruen brought a cup of steaming cocoa and homemade cookies for Nancy, while she and Mr. Drew had second cups of coffee.

"First I'll tell my story," Nancy said, "then I want to hear about your warning, Hannah."

She was interrupted many times by her astonished listeners, and all three agreed that Mr. Jemitt's actions seemed very suspicious. Between him and the greedy relatives, Asa Sidney was in a bad spot.

Finally Mr. Drew said, "What were you saying about a warning?"

Nancy replied, "When I phoned Hannah, she said, 'Asa Sidney! Now you're in for trouble!' Then the phone went dead. What did you mean, Hannah?"

"Well, it's a long story," Mrs. Gruen cautioned. "This isn't serious trouble, but it may mean a heartache for you, Nancy. I'm afraid Bess's and George's parents didn't intend that you find out about the family skeleton."

"But," Nancy protested, "they thought it was all right for Bess and George to take me to the inn to investigate."

The housekeeper sighed. "You never can tell about people. Well, I'll begin at the beginning. I heard this long ago from a woman who used to work for the Sidneys." Hannah repeated the story Asa Sidney had told the girls and added, "Ever since the little girl's death, the Boontons and the Sidneys have been enemies. The Boontons are mad at the Sidneys because Asa didn't pay attention to his family, and the Sidneys are mad at the Boontons because Mrs. Sidney left her husband."

"And Bess Marvin and George Fayne are related to the Boontons, aren't they?" Mr. Drew inquired.

"Exactly! Mrs. Asa Sidney's maiden name was Boonton."

After Mrs. Gruen had explained the complicated family tree, Nancy remarked, "So Bess and George are great-grandnieces of old Asa Sidney!"

"That's it." Hannah nodded. "Mrs. Marvin and Mrs. Fayne didn't expect you to find out all about the feud—only whether or not the Jemitts are mistreating Asa Sidney."

Nancy laughed. "I'll stick strictly to the Jemitt case."

"Once," said Mrs. Gruen, "there was some sort of reconciliation between a Boonton and a Sidney, and a marriage, I believe. But the feelings of both families were so bitter that they disowned the couple. I don't know what happened to them."

At that moment the telephone rang. Nancy leaped to her feet, hoping the call would be from Ned Nickerson, her favorite date.

Instead of Ned's cheery baritone, the voice on the wire proved to be feminine. "Is this Nancy Drew?"

"Yes."

"The Miss Drew who was at The Twisted Candles this afternoon during the storm?"

Nancy's pulse quickened. "Yes, I was there with two friends," she said. "Who is this?"

"Carol Wipple."

"Carol, I'm so glad to hear from you. I was just telling my father of our meeting, and telling him, too, that I hoped to visit you again soon."

"That's good of you, Nancy. I—you—your father's a lawyer, isn't he?"

"Yes."

"Mr. Sidney wants a lawyer, a really good one, Nancy," Carol said. "Could your father come tomorrow morning to draw a new will for him?"

"I'm sure he'll come," said Nancy, "but let me ask him."

A moment later she had his promise and Carol was delighted. "Please come with him. I'll be waiting for you."

"I'll try," Nancy replied. She hurried back to her father. "May I go along?"

"Hm! This is strictly cut-and-dried legal business," Mr. Drew replied, "but then I might need a detective. Okay, come along."

Early the next morning father and daughter were riding southward on the state highway, with Nancy at the wheel of her convertible. The fallen tree had been removed, so she was able to drive directly to The Sign of the Twisted Candles.

"That's the tower room up there," Nancy pointed out. "And I see Carol sweeping the porch."

Carol looked up as the car swung into the driveway, and ran forward to greet Nancy. She acknowledged the introduction to Mr. Drew and thanked him for coming.

"Mr. Sidney is expecting you," she said. "Nancy, you'll show your father the way up, won't you? I must hurry with my work."

"Indeed I will," Nancy stated, opening the door. Then she leaned toward Carol and whispered, "Stay where I can find you. I'll be down in a minute."

Carol nodded and Nancy entered the hallway with her father.

Before they could proceed, Mrs. Jemitt popped

into the hall. "You wish breakfast?" she said. "We don't usually serve this early." She gave no indication that she recognized Nancy.

"No, thank you," Mr. Drew answered. "I have a business appointment with Mr. Sidney."

Mrs. Jemitt jumped in front of the staircase. "You can't see him! He's—he's ill. He didn't sleep well."

"That's all the more reason why I should go up," the lawyer persisted.

Mrs. Jemitt was firm. She stretched out her arms to bar the way. "You'd better leave," she advised angrily.

Nancy was in a quandary. She knew her father would never touch the woman. If Mrs. Jemitt was to be forcibly removed from the stairway, she would have to do it!

CHAPTER V

Buried Chest

WITH the speed of a panther Nancy grabbed Mrs. Jemitt's arms and swung her around out of the way. Then, crying "Come on, Dad!" she ran up the steps two at a time.

Her father followed, leaving Mrs. Jemitt muttering below. Nancy rapped on the door of Asa Sidney's tower room. The old man called to them to enter.

"Ah, Miss Drew, I can't confuse you this bright morning with a musty old painting. Mr. Drew, how are you, sir? Please excuse me for not rising. I am somewhat weak today after a tempestuous night. Draw up a chair."

"Don't disturb yourself, Mr. Sidney." The lawyer placed his bulging brief case on the table and pulled a chair close to the old man's seat. "Mrs. Jemitt said you were ill."

Mr. Sidney frowned. "How would she know? She hasn't been near me nor has Jemitt. Carol brought up my breakfast.

"Well, let's get down to business. I wish to make a new will," the old man said. "Please understand that despite my dowdy surroundings, I am prepared to meet your fee, Mr. Drew. I want the best legal advice, and I can afford to pay for it."

Nancy stepped quietly from the room and closed the door behind her. She paused on the first step to glance out the small window that gave a minimum of light to the stairway. The corner of an old barn was visible. Beyond this was the edge of a forest that grew denser and taller as it stretched toward some hills.

A movement below attracted her attention. Frank Jemitt, dressed in overalls, was coming from the inn. He carried a shovel and a large covered basket which seemed to be very heavy, and kept looking around furtively.

"He certainly acts suspicious," Nancy thought.

Jemitt paused close to the barn, which was at the end of the property farthest from the road. The man looked about him, studied the windows of the house carefully, and then began to dig quickly.

"He's going to bury something!" Nancy speculated.

The hole satisfied Jemitt before it was much more than eighteen inches deep and about as wide. He reached into the basket and took out a small chest.

Nancy gasped. She was sure it was the one marked *Private property of Asa Sidney* which she had seen in the tower room the preceding night!

The chest was about a foot square and eight or ten inches in depth. It was made of ebony and strengthened by brass straps and studs of the same material. Evidently Jemitt knew its contents were valuable.

"What's in it?" Nancy asked herself. "Valuable papers perhaps, or silver? Asa Sidney may have some fine old antique pieces."

Nancy was puzzled. If Jemitt was stealing the chest, why bury it? Why not take it away and sell the contents?

Jemitt dropped the box into the hole and dragged some logs over it from a nearby woodpile. Then he carefully scooped up all the earth dug from the hole, put it into his basket, and scattered it in the woods. Then he went toward the house.

"There's more going on at this place than one sees at a glance," Nancy thought. "I'm sure Asa Sidney didn't ask Jemitt to hide that chest." She continued on downstairs.

When Nancy reached the second floor, Carol was coming from one of the bedrooms. Evidently she had been waiting for Nancy.

"Hello," she said in a subdued voice.

Nancy sensed that Carol had something to tell

"He certainly acts suspicious," Nancy thought

her, but did not know how to begin. She gave the girl an opening.

"Mr. Sidney must have decided very suddenly to make a new will," she remarked.

"Hush!" Carol whispered, looking cautiously about. "I didn't say anything to Father or Mother Jemitt about it. I—I— Oh, Nancy, I'm so worried and upset."

"Why, Carol?" Nancy asked.

"I wish I could get it all straight in my mind." The girl sighed. "I love old Mr. Sidney. He's so friendless and pathetic.

"Last night, right after you left, a man came to see him—some relative who's been here before, usually late at night, but Father would never let him go upstairs. But this time he went up, anyway. A little while afterward, another man came and he too insisted upon going up.

"The most terrible argument broke out between the two men. We could hear them shouting way downstairs in the kitchen. Father Jemitt crept up and listened outside the door.

"The arguments would die down and then break out again. After about an hour the second caller left. He caught Father Jemitt eavesdropping and scolded him terribly. A few minutes later the other man left, slamming the door behind him."

Nancy frowned. "Poor Mr. Sidney! No wonder he said he'd had a tempestuous night."

"Did you know," Carol went on, "that there's some kind of family feud between Mr. Sidney's wife's family and his own relatives?"

"I suspected so," Nancy replied, but did not give any details. "Go on with your story, Carol."

"Father Jemitt was very angry at having been discovered. When he came downstairs he ordered me to bed. But I could hear poor Mr. Sidney pacing the floor, so finally I went up to see him.

"He said to me, 'Carol, will you call Mr. Drew? I want to make a new will.' He asked me to make the appointment secretly. I am— Oh, Nancy, I can't tell you."

"Never mind, then. You must do as you are requested," Nancy said. "But I wonder what Mr. and Mrs. Jemitt will think when they find out."

"Mother Jemitt left the house to walk to the bus right after you came," Carol explained. "Father Jemitt gave me orders that he was not to be disturbed. He's working out in the garage, making some repairs on our car."

"When will Mrs. Jemitt be home?" Nancy asked.

"She is home!" said a harsh voice behind her.

They shrank back in alarm. To Carol's horror and Nancy's surprise, the innkeeper's wife had flung open the door of a nearby room. She held a hairbrush in her hand.

"Carol, you nasty little tattletale!" the woman shouted. "You had better be more sure of my whereabouts before you start blabbing family affairs to strangers!"

The angry woman thrust her scrawny neck out toward Carol and waved the brush menacingly.

"I heard every word you said, you impudent brat! And as for you, young lady," she said to Nancy, "the idea of your gossiping with this simple-minded girl is more than I'll take!"

Nancy leveled her calm blue eyes on the irate woman. For a moment Mrs. Jemitt faltered. Then, regaining her courage, the woman burst out again into a bitter tirade.

"For six years we've worked and slaved to make a home for Carol, and this is our reward!"

Carol cowered against Nancy, and her thin body quivered.

"If you act like a two-year-old you'll have to be treated like one," Mrs. Jemitt cried, hitting Carol on the shoulder with the back of the brush.

The girl gave a cry of pain as the brush descended again, this time on her knuckles. Nancy's face turned white with mingled disgust and anger.

"Stop!" she said, at the same time pulling Carol out of her foster mother's reach and jumping in front of the girl.

Mrs. Jemitt's eyes blazed. "Who are you to come interfering with a mother correcting a wayward child? The nerve of you! Why, you're only a youngster yourself!"

"You certainly are proving yourself unfit to take a mother's place," Nancy replied evenly.

Choking with rage, Mrs. Jemitt lashed out at Nancy, striking her on the arm with the brush. She raised her hand again to repeat the blow, but Nancy deftly caught the woman's wrist and wrenched the hairbrush from her.

"I could have you arrested for that," she said.

"Who do you think you are?" sneered Mrs. Jemitt, but she made no attempt to take the brush, perhaps fearing that Nancy might use it!

"Who I am makes no difference, so far as your attacking me goes," Nancy replied.

"We'll see about that," the woman said. "This is my house and I can run it as I see fit, and that includes getting rid of intruders!"

Nancy answered without flinching, "This is not your house, and I am not an intruder!"

Mrs. Jemitt's jaw dropped. "Wh-what do you mean?" she stammered.

"This house belongs to Asa Sidney and I am here at his invitation."

"Who are you then, if you know everything?" the woman demanded.

"My name is Nancy Drew. Carson Drew is my father. Perhaps you've heard of him?"

"Carson Drew—the lawyer?" Mrs. Jemitt's arrogance suddenly vanished. "His name is in the papers all the time—and I've seen yours there, too. I didn't know who you were. I'm sorry I hit you. You won't tell your father, will you?" she begged. "I'll do anything to make amends."

"I'll make a bargain with you," Nancy said. "I won't tell my father if you'll promise not to harm Carol."

"I promise."

Nancy walked downstairs with the speechless Carol following. The young detective seated herself in the center of one of the empty dining rooms and motioned the other girl to take a chair.

Then, in a low voice, Nancy asked, "What is *really* troubling you?"

Carol began to speak, then closed her mouth. Nancy knew she would have to do some prodding.

"Are you suspicious, Carol, that the Jemitts are not completely honest?"

Carol gave a start. "Nancy, how did you guess?"

CHAPTER VI

An Important Errand

NANCY urged Carol to talk quickly before they might be interrupted.

The girl seemed hesitant to say more. "Oh, Nancy, I wish I were as smart as you. Everything seems so clear to you. To me it's all a muddle."

"Nonsense," Nancy replied. "Just tell me whatever comes into your mind."

"All right. But it's difficult. Maybe I'd better talk about myself first. I'm an orphan—I guess you gathered that from what Mother Jemitt said. I know nothing about my parents. I was found in a church when I was two years old. The authorities couldn't locate any of my family, so I was sent to an orphanage. I lived there until I was ten years old when the Jemitts took me.

"I've worked hard for them. Every day after school I would come home to find dishes and clothes piled up for me to wash. As soon as the law

43

allowed me to leave school they made me stay home. Mr. Sidney urged them to let me go on, but they wouldn't do it. I don't think I owe the Jemitts anything. I've paid my way.

"Mr. Sidney was always nice to me, but after the Jemitts practically forced him to stay in the tower by telling him he wasn't well and that he'd fall if he tried to come downstairs, they began to make me work harder and never let me go anywhere."

"That's a shame," said Nancy. "Was it after Mr. Sidney stayed upstairs that you first suspected Mr. Jemitt of not being fair?"

"Yes."

Carol, warmed by the new friendship, leaned toward Nancy, her eyes round with excitement. "I'm pretty sure that Father Jemitt is robbing Mr. Sidney. I've seen him sneaking around mysteriously and going to town with packages. After that he suddenly seems to have a lot of money, much more than this restaurant brings in. Of course I—"

"That's very interesting," Nancy said loudly. "Once we had some baby robins in a vine outside a bedroom window, too. Do you have many wrens?"

Carol's mouth opened wide in astonishment.

"Good morning, miss!" said a man's voice.

Carol gulped. The voice was that of Frank Jemitt, and at once she understood why Nancy had suddenly interrupted her conversation with the strange remark about birds.

"Have you been served?" Jemitt asked, approaching the table. "Carol, get up and bring the young lady a glass of water!"

"Oh, please don't bother." Nancy smiled, restraining Carol. "I wasn't planning to eat lunch so early."

Jemitt pulled a chair from an adjoining table and prepared to join the conversation.

"You live hereabouts?" he asked Nancy.

"In River Heights," she answered. "I came back this morning with my father, whom Mr. Sidney wished to consult."

"Oh, are you Dr. Crosby's daughter?" Jemitt asked. "I knew he had a beautiful daughter, but I didn't dream—"

"I don't know Dr. Crosby," Nancy put in. "My father is Carson Drew."

Frank Jemitt's face turned a shade paler, and he swallowed heavily.

"Carson Drew—he's upstairs?" he asked.

"Yes, he's been there for over an hour now," Nancy replied coolly. "It must be an important consultation."

"I'm sure it can't be— I mean yes, it must be," Jemitt stammered, rising hurriedly. "Er—excuse me." The agitated man fled from the room.

Nancy watched his retreat with amusement. She wondered if he *was* a thief, and perhaps afraid

Mr. Sidney had discovered that he was dishonest and was going to take action?

"I never saw Father Jemitt so upset," Carol commented. "He seems to be scared of your father."

"Which would confirm your suspicions and mine," Nancy remarked. "I think I'll keep an eye on Mr. Jemitt."

"Oh dear! I've talked too much." Carol sighed. "Maybe I'm all wrong."

At that moment Nancy heard her father's footsteps on the stairway. She arose and hurried to the hall.

"Are you ready to go?" she asked.

"No," Mr. Drew replied. "Mr. Sidney's case is strange and complicated. After what I've heard, I shall not leave this house until the document is witnessed by someone competent to stand up under a grueling trial in court."

He went into the hall telephone booth and made a call. Nancy saw him frown, and in a minute came out, looking disappointed.

"The man I want to reach will be out for half an hour. I didn't want to give the message to anyone else. Nancy, I guess you'll have to help me. Speed is essential. Will you drive to the Smith's Ferry branch of the River Heights National Bank and ask for Mr. Hill—Raymond Hill? He's the executive vice president.

"Tell Mr. Hill I want him to come back here

with you to witness an important document. I'm well acquainted with him, and I'm sure he will grant me this favor. Remember, the sooner you get back with him the better."

"I'll go at once," Nancy replied, excited by the new element of mystery.

She ran back to the table and told Carol that she had to go on an important errand for her father, but that she would return shortly.

As Nancy was talking, she saw the swinging door which led to the kitchen move slightly. Someone was listening.

"I think I'll go out this way, it's shorter," she said abruptly, skipping across to the kitchen door and suddenly pushing it ajar. As she had expected, the door did not open far, and there was a muttered exclamation from behind it.

"Oh, I'm so sorry! Did I hit somebody?" Nancy asked.

Mrs. Jemitt was revealed, looking rather dazed and rubbing her ear. "No, not much," she said sarcastically.

The woman wheeled about, darted through the kitchen, and vanished into the garden. Nancy was at her heels, but Mr. Drew called her back.

"You were a little too fast for me." He smiled. "I just wanted to tell you that Peter Boonton and Jacob Sidney, the two men you told me about, are coming here this morning. We want the will signed and witnessed before they arrive. That's the reason I'm asking for the greatest possible speed."

Nancy nodded and left the house. She saw Jemitt, who seemed to be having difficulty starting his automobile. His wife, her back to Nancy, was beside the car talking and gesticulating violently to him.

"She's probably telling him about my errand," Nancy thought, "so I must hurry. On the other hand, I may never have another opportunity to look at that buried box. I must find out if it belongs to Asa Sidney."

Out of sight of the Jemitts, she ran to the barn. It took only a moment to roll away the logs in the improvised woodpile and uncover what Jemitt had buried underneath.

"If it's what I think, I'm sure Dad would want me to take the chest to the bank," the young sleuth told herself.

The loose dirt was easy to brush aside, and anxiety gave Nancy added strength. She saw at a glance that the chest was indeed the one with the carved twisted candles, and marked *Private property of Asa Sidney*. She lifted it out.

Lugging the heavy ebony and brass chest, Nancy went around the far corner of the house and climbed into her car. She started the motor, locked the doors, and sped off.

The highway ahead was clear. Nancy glanced into her rear-vision mirror to see if anyone was on the road behind. What she had feared was true. Frank Jemitt's big car had lurched into the road and was roaring after her!

"Does he know where I'm going, and why?" she thought.

Jemitt's car, although left behind by Nancy's first burst of speed, began to crawl up.

"There's no doubt about it, he's after me," Nancy told herself. "Either he's going to prevent my bringing Mr. Hill, or force me to give up the stolen chest!"

CHAPTER VII

The Race

THE convertible sped along as fast as Nancy dared go. But Jemitt's more powerful car was slowly catching up. Would he force her off the road? A second glimpse in the rear-view mirror disclosed Carol's foster father crouched over the wheel of his car, his teeth clenched, his face red.

"If I can only reach the turn to Smith's Ferry," Nancy thought, "maybe I can outwit him."

Calculating her speed and the road with precision, she pretended to pass the intersecting highway. Then, with a quick twist of the wheel she shot into the fork. The low-slung convertible hugged the road and with squealing tires made the sharp curve safely.

Nancy slowed down a moment to glance behind her. A look of relief spread over her face.

Jemitt had fallen into the trap. Nancy's abrupt turn had caught him unawares, and he had shot ahead in the direction of River Heights. When he jammed on his brakes, the speeding car skidded off the road into a small ditch.

"Sorry, Mr. Jemitt." Nancy grinned.

In a short time she was driving up the main street of Smith's Ferry at a sedate pace. She found the bank without difficulty and parked, then picked up the chest and entered the building.

"I should like to speak with Mr. Hill—Mr. Raymond Hill," Nancy told the woman receptionist.

"Do you have an appointment?"

"No, but if you'll tell him I'm here for Carson Drew on important business, I'm sure he'll see me," Nancy replied.

The woman smiled and went off. Presently she returned and ushered her into Mr. Hill's office. The pleasant bank officer was about Carson Drew's age.

"What can I do for your father, Nancy?" he asked. "Oh, don't be surprised that I know your name. I am no detective, but I've seen your picture on your father's office desk, so I recognized you immediately."

Nancy smiled, then explained, "Dad would like you to witness an important document over which there may be some legal trouble. If it is convenient for you now, I'll drive you to where Dad is waiting. It's a matter in which minutes are precious, Mr. Hill."

"Then I'll come at once," the banker replied.

"But first," said Nancy, "I'd like to have this chest put in a safe place."

"I'll have it placed in the vault," Mr. Hill said, pressing a button to summon a clerk. "I'll give you a receipt."

A man in a uniform appeared in response to the summons. Mr. Hill gave him the box with instructions to place it in the bank's vault.

"You fill in this receipt," he told Nancy, handing her a form. She wrote a brief but accurate description of the chest, and Mr. Hill signed the paper.

"Now let's go," he said.

He accompanied Nancy to her car and she headed it toward the Sidney mansion. Mr. Hill leaned back in the seat without speaking, although his eyes traveled nervously from time to time to the speedometer.

"Look out!" he suddenly exclaimed.

They had just reached the intersecting highway when a car pulled across it. As Nancy deftly skirted the slow-moving and mud-splattered automobile she noted that the driver was Frank Jemitt.

"He must have damaged his car when he went into that ditch," she thought, pulling ahead.

A glance in the mirror showed Jemitt shaking both fists over his head at her retreating car.

Nancy chuckled and briefly explained to Mr. Hill about the caretaker.

A few minutes later she turned into the driveway of The Sign of the Twisted Candles and swung to a stop at the porch steps.

"I'm not being kidnapped, am I?" Mr. Hill joked as he got out. "What is this place, and where is Mr. Drew?"

As if in answer to his question the lawyer stepped onto the porch and greeted the banker.

"You made excellent time," he said to Nancy. "I scarcely expected you to have reached Smith's Ferry yet. None of the interference we have feared has made its appearance yet."

Mr. Hill followed the lawyer into the house. Nancy remained outside and sat down on the steps to mull over recent events. She speculated on what Jemitt would say to her when he arrived, and wished she knew what had made her father so concerned about Asa Sidney's affairs.

"I wonder if it affects Carol in any way," she pondered. "Wouldn't it be great if he left her some money in his will!"

The idea was driven from Nancy's mind by the approach of a car turning into the roadway of the inn.

"Here comes trouble," she said to herself.

For a moment Nancy thought it might be Jemitt's car, but it proved to be Jacob Sidney's sedan.

Directly behind it was the car belonging to Peter Boonton.

Jacob Sidney jumped out and sprinted for the porch. Peter Boonton stepped down hurriedly and dashed after him.

Nancy had leaped to her feet and crossed the porch. Pretending to stumble, she now leaned against the front door for support. Boonton and his rival, panting heavily, drew up side by side in front of her.

"Stand aside and see that no one follows me!" Peter Boonton commanded.

"Nothing of the kind!" Jacob Sidney shouted. "I was here first. Listen, miss, I'm in a hurry to see Mr. Sidney on a confidential matter. Let me in!"

"He's busy just now," Nancy said. "He's in conference and doesn't wish to be disturbed. Won't you sit down?" She pointed toward the porch chairs.

"With whom is he conferring?" Boonton demanded.

"I'm not at liberty to discuss that," Nancy replied. "Won't you two gentlemen have some tea?"

"Two gentlemen!" Jacob Sidney sneered. "I can account for only one here."

"Thank you for the compliment, Sidney," Boonton retorted. "I'm glad you admit you're no gentleman."

"Don't speak to me, you—you double-crosser!"

Sidney fumed. "I'll have you understand that you and I are not on speaking terms!"

Boonton turned to Nancy. "Who are you?"

"Why, Mr. Boonton, we were introduced last night," Nancy replied. "Bess and George were here with me, don't you recall?"

"I remember you!" Sidney exclaimed. "You were in a car down where the tree fell. Say, what's your business at this place?"

"See here, Sidney," Boonton yelled, "you're just trying to keep me from going upstairs! I can see through your tricks!"

"I'll go up first because I'm his blood relative, and bear his name," Sidney shouted.

He suddenly pushed Nancy aside and jerked open the door. With a strangled cry Boonton caught his rival by the coat and the two men leaped into the hallway together, Nancy at their heels.

A new obstacle confronted them, however, and Nancy felt like giving Carol Wipple three cheers. Across the bottom step of the stairs she had stretched a broom and a mop. Many of the treads were dripping soapy water, and halfway up knelt Carol, surrounded by three buckets of water.

"Hey! Let us up!" Boonton shouted.

Carol gave a start and upset one pail. The men leaped to one side just as a cascade of dirty water splashed down upon the spot where they had been standing.

"Oh, you scared me!" Carol cried, while Nancy suppressed a chuckle. "Wait, and I'll mop the water so you can come up without slipping."

While the two men fairly danced with impatience, Carol carried down one pail of water, then climbed the stairs again and carried another to the top. Then slowly she wiped away the excess water.

Her skirt was soaked and her hands red, but Carol seemed to be enjoying herself. She picked up the broom and mop, then the two men made a rush for the stairs.

They jammed together, clawing at each other for a moment. At last Boonton gained the advantage and darted upward, Sidney only a step behind.

"Carol, you were superb!" Nancy whispered, hugging the girl. "It gave Asa Sidney and Dad another precious five minutes."

The young detective raced up the steps after the two men. She reached them just as they burst into the tower room.

CHAPTER VIII

Eavesdropper

"IN the name of the law I demand that you stop!" Peter Boonton shouted as he entered the tower room.

"Don't pay any attention to him!" Jacob Sidney answered coolly.

Nancy saw Asa Sidney in his favorite chair near the great twisted candle. Standing at a nearby table was Carson Drew, staring calmly over his shoulder at the intruders. Raymond Hill was seated at the table, a pen in his hand. Apparently he had just finished using it because he capped the pen and returned it to his pocket.

"What branch of the law do you represent?" Mr. Drew asked the newcomers, gathering up the papers.

Boonton stood stock-still, his mouth opening and closing. "I—I'm not an officer," he said finally. "But hasn't a relative any rights in a case like this?"

"A case like what?" Mr. Drew asked. "I've just finished drawing Mr. Asa Sidney's will, which Mr. Hill, here, has witnessed. Is there anything illegal about that?"

"I demand to see the document," Jacob Sidney announced, striding forward, "to be sure this is the document of a person who is mentally sound."

"I assure you it is," the lawyer said, somewhat annoyed.

Jacob spoke up. "We don't want any ideas put into this old man's head."

The remark angered Nancy. Her father's code of justice was rigid and unyielding. Her blue eyes flashing, she said, "Mr. Sidney, I think you owe my father an apology and Mr. Asa Sidney too!"

Jacob Sidney gave an ingratiating smile. "Little spitfire, eh? Who are you, anyhow? Everybody seems to be running this show except those who should be."

Angry, Asa Sidney arose and faced his relatives. "Why is it," he said, "that you have left me alone for over two years, and have suddenly become concerned about my mental condition and my affairs? Is it because you suspect that I won't last long and you want my money? I assure you I am just as able to take care of my own business today as I was two years ago."

"I don't doubt it, Uncle Asa," Jacob Sidney

said in mollifying tones. "I just want to warn you against putting too much confidence in strangers."

"And not only strangers, but scheming relatives," Peter Boonton interjected. "You must know that *I* have your best interests at heart, Uncle Asa."

"Just the same," said the old man, "a stranger may prove to be a great friend." He clapped Nancy on the shoulder, finally letting his arm rest there affectionately.

He turned to his nephews. "When I need your advice I'll send for you," he said testily.

"I was only trying to help," Jacob muttered.

"Do you really wish to be of service to me?" Asa asked, a twinkle in his eyes.

"Yes, indeed," Jacob replied, eager to ingratiate himself with the old man.

"Let me do it," Peter offered, thrusting himself forward.

"Well, you may both do it," Asa said, stroking his long beard.

"What shall we do?" chorused the nephews.

"Get out!" Asa thundered in a tone that surprised everyone. "Get out of here and stay out until I ask you to come back! You've sickened me, both of you. You think I have money and you're fluttering around me like a pair of vultures waiting for me to die! Go!"

His nephews paled at their schemes being exposed like this before the lawyer, the banker and, most of all, before a young girl. Nancy felt Asa's hand tremble as it rested on her shoulder. He swayed as he clung for a moment to her arm to steady himself.

His nephews backed toward the door. Nancy feared that another outburst from old Asa would seriously sap his feeble strength, so she slipped toward the door to speed the men's departure.

"Please be calm and reasonable," Peter Boonton said in a low, soothing tone. "I was impetuous, and I beg you to bear me no ill will, Uncle."

Asa wearily signaled to Nancy to open the door. She grasped the knob and swung the door inward.

"Oh!" she exclaimed.

Frank Jemitt was crouched just outside!

"I—I dropped something. I—I—I—" he stammered. The innkeeper stared at Nancy and the others in dismay.

"I—I dropped something," he repeated. "It was when I was cleaning this morning."

"You were eavesdropping," Boonton said, advancing toward the man.

"Never!" Jemitt wailed. "I wouldn't do such a thing!"

He teetered for a moment on the top step, then with a yell of fright toppled over and rolled headlong down the stairs. He picked himself up on the landing.

"Are—are you hurt?" Nancy gasped.

"I'll sue you, Boonton, for causing me to lose my balance!" Jemitt shouted, rubbing his head and one shin. "I might have broken my neck!"

"Frank," Asa called, "when you get all the way down, open the front door for these two gentlemen."

All but Peter and Jacob smiled. The two men silently descended the stairway.

As they vanished, Asa Sidney sighed deeply. "I hope they never return."

"I'll tell you a secret about your family," said Nancy. "They're not all like your nephews. The two girls who were here with me to celebrate your birthday are Bess Marvin and George Fayne."

"Well, well," Asa Sidney said, a smile coming over his face, "I'm glad to hear there are a few charming people in my family tree."

Mr. Hill said he must return to the bank. He shook hands with Asa Sidney, then spoke to Nancy's father.

"I didn't know that acting as witness to the signing of a will could become such an interesting adventure. . . . And, Carson, I'll certainly remember all you told me at our little conference. Is there anything further?"

"No, I'm sure you understand the general situation as well as I do," Mr. Drew replied. "Shall Nancy drive you back to the bank?"

"No, that won't be necessary," Mr. Hill said. "I'll phone my chauffeur who is no doubt waiting there for me, and have him come here. It must be very close to lunchtime."

"I don't have to consult my watch to agree with you." Mr. Drew smiled. "How about you, Nancy?"

"I could eat—indeed I could! But I can wait, too."

"Good! I want to question Jemitt," her father said. "Well, then, good-by for the present, Raymond."

As he left the tower, and Mr. Drew paused in the doorway for another word with old Mr. Sidney, soft footfalls were heard on the stairs. Carol appeared, carrying a loaded tray.

"I—I made some sandwiches," she said shyly. "And a pitcher of cocoa."

"Wonderful! Wonderful!" the lawyer exclaimed. "And you must eat with us, Carol. I should like to become better acquainted with you."

"Carol is a very good girl, my only comfort and helper," Asa Sidney said. "My dear child, sit here beside me. You look very tired."

"I'm not tired, really," the young waitress replied stoutly, putting the tray on the table and lifting the cloth that covered it. "Now, please help yourselves. I can't stay, because some people have arrived and I must serve them."

She hurried off and the others began to eat.

When they finished, Nancy said, "Did Mr. Hill tell you men about the chest I put in the bank vault?"

"No," they answered.

"Mr. Sidney," Nancy went on, "did you ask Mr. Jemitt to bury your chest that used to be under that table?" She pointed.

The old man looked at the spot in amazement. "Why, no, of course not. What do you know about it?"

Nancy told her story and added, "I hope I did the right thing. Anyway, here is the receipt." She took it from her handbag and handed it to Mr. Sidney.

"You certainly used your head," the old man told her. "Thanks." Then he chuckled. "Outwitting Jemitt, who's three times your age, is an accomplishment. You're proud of her, aren't you, Mr. Drew?"

The lawyer looked grave. "This is a very serious matter, Nancy. I'm relieved that everything turned out all right, but I think we should ask Jemitt for an explanation of his action."

He went downstairs and a few minutes later returned with the manager of The Twisted Candles. Frank Jemitt was told about the chest.

A look of fright came over his face for the fraction of a second, then he said smoothly, "Sure I took the chest. Mr. Sidney slept later than usual and I was afraid those conniving relatives of his would come up here and steal it. I assume the contents are valuable?"

Asa Sidney did not reply. He seemed to be lost in thought.

Nancy and her father exchanged glances. They doubted Jemitt's story but had to admit his motive might have been an honest one.

"All right, Frank," Asa Sidney said finally, "I accept your explanation, but don't take anything more out of this house."

The innkeeper bowed and without a word hurried off.

Asa Sidney said to the Drews, "There are valuable papers and some silver pieces in the chest." Nancy had speculated correctly. After a pause he added, "I realize I am at a great disadvantage being up here alone. Perhaps I depend too much on Carol to keep me informed on the management downstairs."

Nancy thought, "And Carol's too considerate to upset him by telling about the way she's treated and the run-down condition of the inn."

A faraway look came into the old man's eyes. "It is my turn to reveal a secret. My memory isn't what it used to be. My dear wife and I had camouflaged cupboards built in this house and hid many things of hers and mine in them, but I've forgotten where they are. She took hers away. Let's hope the rest haven't been found and stolen. I hereby appoint you, Nancy, and Carol—and your friends Bess and George—to do some searching. But one word of caution. It must be done without the knowledge of the Jemitts."

"Oh, I'd love that!" Nancy exclaimed. "Okay, Dad?" Her father nodded approval and she grinned happily. "But I'll have to eat an awful lot of meals here and call on you very often to make my sleuthing look natural."

"Remember," the old man warned, "secrecy! Secrecy!"

CHAPTER IX

Doubtful Friendship

MR. DREW said he would meet Nancy downstairs —he wanted to speak to Frank Jemitt before leaving. His daughter lingered to ask Asa Sidney a few questions.

"Please tell me which bedroom you and your wife used to occupy."

"The master bedroom at the east end of the hall overlooking the driveway."

"Do the Jemitts use it now?" Nancy queried.

"No, they've taken one at the west end. Carol's is opposite theirs. Mine and two others used to be given to travelers, but no guests have been here for a couple of years. Emma said the place was making enough money without it."

Nancy made no comment. Instead she asked, "Would there be any special way to identify the hiding places of the articles?"

"Oh yes. By the design of a twisted candle. It is also on boxes and chests."

"That will make it easy," Nancy said.

With a sudden feeling of affection and pity for the old man, she kissed him and said good-by, promising to start her search the next day.

At the front porch Nancy came upon another dramatic scene and stepped back a couple of feet into the hall so as not to intrude. Her father was talking to Frank Jemitt, whose back was against an open window in the dining room.

"What was your income from the pastureland last year?" Mr. Drew was saying.

"Only about two hundred dollars."

"Did you give Mr. Sidney an accounting of it?"

"I spent the money fixing up the place."

"In general repairs to the building, or in the restaurant equipment?" Mr. Drew asked.

"I—I forget," Jemitt said, wiping his brow. "General repairs, of course. Sure, that's right."

"The house hasn't been painted," Mr. Drew commented. "The grounds are in bad shape. What improvements did you make?"

"Say, I'm not on the witness stand!" Jemitt snarled. "I'm not going to answer questions you got no business asking. If you think there's anything crooked going on, maybe you're right. Keep an eye on those two guys who were here this morning."

Nancy had stood so quietly that she had not

been noticed by Mrs. Jemitt, who had sneaked in from the kitchen. The woman cautiously took up a position at the window near her husband.

As Mr. Drew paced up and down the porch, Mrs. Jemitt, using the drapery for concealment, whispered something to Mr. Jemitt. He slyly pulled a long envelope from beneath his jacket and held it behind him. His wife's hand reached out and took it.

"Yes, Mr. Drew," Jemitt went on, "and what's more I think each one of those fellows suspects the other of sneaking things out of this house."

Nancy stepped softly from the hall and walked up behind Mrs. Jemitt, who smiled as she glanced at the letter, then turned noiselessly away. On her face was a look of secret triumph, but the expression was quickly wiped away as Nancy confronted her.

"What do you want?" the woman snapped.

"Nothing at all," Nancy said with an innocent air. "I was just looking for an envelope— Oh, you've found it, haven't you?"

"Not at all," Mrs. Jemitt replied, concealing the envelope beneath her apron. "This is for me and it just came in the morning mail."

"Perhaps you made a mistake?" Nancy remarked. "May I look at the address?"

"You may not," Mrs. Jemitt retorted. "I guess a body has a right to some privacy in her own house, even if it is open to the public."

She brushed past Nancy, only to meet Mr. Drew. Attracted by the sharp voices, he had entered the room to investigate.

"What's the trouble?" he asked.

"No trouble at all, thank you," Mrs. Jemitt said. "Just a little misunderstanding."

Nancy spoke up. "I happened to see Mr. Jemitt pass an envelope through the window to his wife, and thought it might—er—be for Mr. Sidney."

Her announcement took Mrs. Jemitt completely by surprise. In her agitation she dropped the envelope, and Nancy swiftly scooped it up.

"There *is* a misunderstanding," she said. "This letter is for Mr. Sidney."

"I was just going to take it up to the old gentleman," the woman said.

"Then I apologize for detaining you." Nancy smiled. "I see it's from the Midwestern Mining Company."

Without another word Mrs. Jemitt took it and hurried upstairs. Nancy, with a wink at her father, followed to be sure it was delivered.

When she came down, Mr. Drew said, "My business here is finished. Let's go!"

As they walked to the car, he continued, "You've just given me some very valuable information, Nancy. Among Mr. Sidney's assets are shares of stock in the mining company. The old man thought they were worthless because he had received no dividends in several years.

"I promised to investigate," the lawyer said, "because I have some of that stock myself and it pays well. I'm sure that envelope contained a dividend check because I've just received one."

"Then you suspect the Jemitts of taking Mr. Sidney's dividend checks and forging the endorsements on them?" Nancy asked as they rode along.

"I'm afraid so," Mr. Drew replied. "It will take time to prove it, though."

"While you're doing that," said Nancy, "I'll start my search in the house for cupboards marked with the sign of a twisted candle." She slid into the driver's seat.

Mr. Drew got out of the car at his office. Nancy, excited by the prospect of going back to the Sidney mansion with Bess and George, went directly to the Marvin home. To her dismay, she saw Peter Boonton's car at the curb.

"Oh dear! I don't want to meet him," she thought. "Maybe I'd better drive over to the Faynes' and see if George is there."

As she sat debating, Nancy suddenly saw George look out a window directly at her. To Nancy's surprise George did not wave; just stared, then moved out of sight.

"How strange!" Nancy thought. "Something seems to be on George's mind. I'm sure she saw me."

Nancy decided to try seeing the girls, anyway,

and tell them of Asa Sidney's request. She walked to the door.

Bess answered the bell. "Hello, Nancy," she said, stepping outside and closing the door behind her. "Great-Uncle Peter's inside. I hear you were at The Sign of the Twisted Candles again today."

Nancy nodded. "That's what I want to talk to you about, Bess. Call George, will you? I have some exciting things to tell you, and we must go out there tomorrow."

"Oh, I don't think I care to come," Bess replied. "And I'm sure George wouldn't be interested, either."

Nancy flushed with disappointment and embarrassment at Bess's cool retort.

"I—I'm sorry," she said with a lump in her throat. "Dad has been retained as Mr. Sidney's lawyer, and I've been given a job too. Some problems have come up. We'd have fun tackling them together."

"Oh, so your father is really taking sides in the case, is he?" Bess asked frigidly. "I'm sorry, Nancy, but I must go back inside."

Stung by the snub, Nancy ran to her car and drove away, tears brimming in her eyes. What sinister influence in the bitter Boonton-Sidney feud had brought Bess and George to a point of breaking off a lovely friendship?

Nancy drove on and on, lost in thought. Suddenly she realized that the road she had subconsciously chosen led to the Sidney mansion.

"Maybe fate is steering me back there," the young sleuth told herself.

When she arrived at the turn and walked in, no one was around. The Jemitts' car was gone. When Carol did not come out to greet Nancy, apprehension seized her. Had something happened?

She shook off the feeling and ascended the stairs. After all, she had a right to be here—this was a public restaurant. At the top of the stairway she met Carol.

"Nancy!" the girl cried. "Oh, I'm so glad you came back. I have something marvelous to tell you. Right after you left I heard Mr. Sidney's bell ring and rushed up there. He said he'd asked you, Bess, George, and me to do some searching, but that you wouldn't be back until tomorrow, so he wanted me to start. The Jemitts have gone to town.

"Mr. Sidney remembered a false drawer in the bottom of a bureau in the empty master bedroom and had me look there. What do you think I found?"

"Clothes?"

"No."

"Jewelry?"

"You're getting warm. Nancy, it was a diamond bracelet!"

CHAPTER X

A Shocking Summons

"A diamond bracelet!" Nancy gasped. "What did you do with it, Carol?"

"I gave it to Mr. Sidney." She chuckled. "He hid the bracelet under the seat of his chair. Oh, Nancy, it was beautiful lying there in its velvet box."

"What did he say?" Nancy asked.

Carol laughed softly. He said, 'Keep going and bring everything to me before those vultures get my fortune!' Nancy, nobody's in the house. Let's search right now."

Nancy did not need to be urged. First they scoured the master bedroom where the bracelet had been cached. Neither the walls, floor, nor closet yielded any clue to where there might be a camouflaged safe or other kind of hiding place. Next the bed, wardrobe, and other pieces of furniture were searched. They revealed nothing.

73

"Let's try another room," Carol urged.

Nancy glanced at her watch. "It's four o'clock. By any chance did Mrs. Jemitt ask you to prepare food for dinner—like putting a roast in the oven?"

Carol clapped a hand over her mouth. "Oh my goodness! I was supposed to put a leg of lamb in the stove."

Nancy chuckled. "Then you'd better go do it quickly. If Mrs. Jemitt returns and finds you haven't done it—"

Carol fairly flew from the room and down the stairs. Nancy continued the search alone. She walked into what had been the adjoining dressing room. As she gazed around, her eyes were attracted to an ornate wooden panel directly above the mirror of a walnut dressing table. At first glance one might mistake the small square as part of the furniture below it.

At once Nancy noted two unusual features about the panel, which she suspected might be a door: it had no visible way to open it and a series of connecting loops was carved on its face. On a hunch Nancy bent over so she could view the pattern sideways.

"I'm right!" she thought. "It *is* a twisted candle! Something must be hidden behind there. But how do I open that door?"

Nancy gazed at it for fully a minute. Then she

concluded that if a particular spot on the door were pushed, it might release a hidden lock.

Not wishing to be disturbed and fearful the Jemitts might rush in, Nancy went into the bedroom and turned the key in the door to the hall. Then she hastened back and pulled the dressing table aside.

"Oh, I hope I can get this open!"

Nancy was breathing excitedly now. Inch by inch she pressed a thumb over the entire surface. Nothing happened.

"It's tricky," she thought.

Next Nancy tried both thumbs, experimenting with various combinations. Still nothing happened.

"I'm sure I'm not wrong," she murmured. Suddenly she smiled. "The candle, of course. That's the clue!"

This time she ran a finger over the whole design and finally felt a slight protrusion on one of the swirls. She pushed it hard and the panel with the carved candle dropped into her hand. At the rear of the opening was a latch. Quickly she lifted it and a door swung open.

To her surprise a music box inside began to play. Now she could see that it was a highly ornate —and, she guessed, priceless old piece. Dainty dancing figures moved around the top. Nancy was about to lift the music box from its hiding place when there was a knock on the door. Instantly she replaced everything and hurried to open it.

Carol stood there. She whispered, "They're home! You'd better scoot!"

"You're right. Listen, Carol. Tell Mr. Sidney I found a gorgeous music box but didn't have time to take it to him."

"How marvelous! It'll make him very happy."

The two girls rushed down the stairs. Carol ran to the kitchen, while Nancy dashed out the front door. No one was in sight and she drove off quickly.

It was not until she reached home that Nancy recalled Bess's rebuff. Despite the exciting story she had to tell at dinner about her afternoon's search, the diamond bracelet, and the music box, the young sleuth became glum and did not eat much.

"What's happened to your appetite?" Hannah Gruen asked her.

"Nothing."

Mr. Drew regarded her thoughtfully. "Now then, partner!" he said, rising from the table and putting an arm about his daughter's shoulders. "Out with it! Something's bothering you."

"Oh dear! You always know, don't you?" Nancy said with a pensive smile. "Dad, for some reason connected with Asa Sidney's case, George and Bess are angry with me. George won't speak to me at all, and Bess snubbed me this afternoon."

*The panel with the curved candle
dropped into her hand!*

Nancy's lip quivered at the memory.

"Hm!" the lawyer said. "That's too bad." He frowned. "Some people are hard to understand. Why should the Marvins and Faynes poison the minds of their daughters with a family feud so old it concerns none of them? It's pitiful. I don't know how to help you, Nancy. You'll have to accept the situation, I'm afraid, and trust that time will set matters straight."

"I suppose," said Nancy, "that both sides are suspicious of you for being Asa Sidney's counsel, and for that reason George and Bess are forbidden to be friends with me."

Mr. Drew nodded. "You'll have to let events prove that neither you nor I have meddled in the affairs of the family."

"I'm disappointed in George and Bess just the same." Nancy sighed again.

The lawyer looked at his daughter sympathetically and decided that the best way to mend Nancy's hurt feelings was to lead the discussion into other channels.

"I'm afraid Mr. Sidney's case is more complicated than we realize," he remarked. "It's a big puzzle."

Nancy instantly became alert. "What's the trouble?"

"I have a strong hunch there's systematic pilfering that's draining the old man's fortune," her father said.

Nancy asked, "Do you suspect anyone besides the Jemitts? Surely Peter Boonton and Jacob Sidney are not dishonest, no matter how badly they act."

"We can safely rule out Boonton and Sidney," Mr. Drew said.

"Let's call on Asa Sidney tomorrow morning and see what we can find out," Nancy suggested.

That night she slept uneasily. She kept thinking of the big sleuthing job ahead of her and of the problem with Bess and George. At breakfast she ate little. Her father sat lost in thought, with Hannah Gruen hovering over them, coaxing them to try her waffles.

The telephone rang and she went to answer it. Nancy heard Hannah say, "I can't hear you at all! Who is this?"

"I'll take it, Hannah," Nancy said quietly as she hurried into the hall.

"Nancy Drew speaking. Who is this?"

"Oh, Nancy!"

The exclamation came faintly over the wire, ending in a deep, shuddering sigh.

"Hello? Who is this? Who's speaking? What's the matter?"

"Nancy—something—something—"

"Is this Bess? Or George?" Nancy demanded.

"Nancy, this is Carol. Oh, please come at once! Something awful has happened. O-oh!"

There was a sharp click, then silence. Carol had

hung up, leaving Nancy in a state of mingled surprise and alarm. She ran to her father at once, and in a few words repeated what she had heard.

Mr. Drew's face became grave. "We must go there immediately," he said. "I will be ready as soon as you bring your car around in front."

A few minutes later Nancy and her father were on the now-familiar road to The Sign of the Twisted Candles. Few words were exchanged between them, for their minds were intent on the mysterious and urgent summons from Carol.

What could have happened? Nancy thought of a dozen answers. Perhaps Mrs. Jemitt had not kept her promise and had done something cruel to Carol. Perhaps Peter and Jacob had met again, and had joined in a pitched battle.

At last the tower of the old mansion could be seen above the trees, and a minute later Nancy steered into the sweeping driveway.

"Oh!" she gasped, applying the brakes.

An undertaker's long black car was just driving away. Someone was—dead!

Nancy did not wait for her father but ran into the house. She halted at the sight of Carol's huddled form on the bottom step of the big staircase, her head on her knees, her thin shoulders shaking with sobs.

"Carol!" Nancy cried, sitting down beside the girl and clasping her hands. "Tell me what happened."

"Mis-Mister Si-Si-Sidney," Carol said. "He died during the night. I found him—I thought he was asleep—when I brought up his breakfast this morning."

As Mr. Drew walked into the hall, Nancy stated soberly, "Mr. Sidney is dead."

"Too bad," he said with a shake of his head. "I'm sorry. It's true that he lived far, far longer than most persons do, and his life was not a happy one. If only he had lasted a little longer until certain matters could be straightened out, what trouble could have been averted!"

"Why, Dad, what do you mean?" Nancy asked.

"I mean that the bickering relatives will now gather and begin to fight over the estate. Then there are other people who probably have already removed some of his property, reducing the value of the estate."

At this juncture, Frank Jemitt appeared with a long face. "Mr. Sidney has gone to his just reward," the innkeeper intoned.

"I shall stay here as his executor and take charge," Mr. Drew replied simply.

"Who asked you to butt in?" Jemitt snapped, dropping his pretense of sorrow. "There's nothing to be done. Emma and I have made arrangements for the funeral, and we'll even pay for it out of our own pockets!"

"That won't be necessary," the lawyer told him. Nancy noted that Asa Sidney's death seemed to have added to Jemitt's courage—and offensiveness.

Mr. Drew regarded the man keenly. Determined to assume charge of the late Asa Sidney's personal effects, he said evenly:

"Your services will not be needed here much longer, Mr. Jemitt. You are free to make other plans and leave any time after the funeral."

"Is that so? Well, we'll see about that!" Jemitt snapped.

CHAPTER XI

Surprise Inheritance

SHOCKED by Jemitt's complete lack of mourning for a man who had been so kind to him, Nancy, her father, and Carol looked at the innkeeper in disgust.

"I think," said Mr. Drew, "that you had better keep such thoughts to yourself until after Mr. Sidney's will is read. Until then, there is work for you to do. First of all, prepare a sign to put over the one at the entrance. Mark it 'Closed.' Then make a complete list of all the food on hand."

Jemitt answered defiantly, "Why do you think you can give me orders?"

"Because as Mr. Sidney's attorney I am in charge here. I'll need a duplicate set of keys."

The manager stepped back in surprise. "Okay, I'll do what you say. But first my wife and I will clean up the tower room."

At that announcement Nancy squeezed her father's hand as a signal not to leave the couple alone on the third floor. He understood her message.

"Mr. Jemitt, my daughter, and Carol—if she feels able—will accompany you. Do not touch anything but the bedding and towels. I'll join you after I make a few phone calls."

The caretaker's eyelids narrowed to a look of hatred but he kept silent.

"I—I'll be all right," Carol said, rising.

Nancy put an arm about her and they went upstairs together. A quiver ran through the younger girl's body as they entered the tower, but this lasted only a moment. The Jemitts arrived almost immediately. Instead of confining their work to the bed and bathroom, they began mopping and dusting. It was soon evident that they were doing more snooping than cleaning.

Fearful that the Jemitts would find the hidden bracelet, Nancy finally spoke up. "My father did not ask you to do this," she said.

"Humph!" the woman exclaimed. "And what does he know about cleaning?" She went on with her work.

"Stop!" Nancy ordered. "Carol, run down and tell my father to come right up here."

As Carol started from the room, Jemitt said, "Oh, all right. Emma, take the linen and blanket off the bed." As she did, Nancy saw him lift a corner of the mattress and peer underneath.

Realizing his action had been detected, Jemitt quickly straightened up and went to get the towels from an adjacent bathroom. By this time Mr. Drew had arrived and instantly Jemitt and his wife vanished down the stairway.

But the Drews heard Jemitt shout back, "Carol, don't you dare take any more orders from Nancy Drew or her father! We're your foster parents and you'll do as we say! Right now get to work on our bedrooms."

Nancy sighed. "Dad, isn't it frightful?"

He nodded. "I see more trouble ahead, but two things we must do: protect Carol and take care of this old mansion. Nancy, do you think Hannah would be willing to come here and stay with you?"

"Oh, Dad, I'm sure she would, and I'm glad that you want me to stay."

The lawyer smiled. "I think Carol needs you." A few minutes later several relatives arrived, saying Jemitt had phoned them. Nancy was glad Bess and George were not among them, because she did not feel equal to coping with that unhappy situation at this time. Mrs. Fayne and Mrs. Marvin came with Peter Boonton. They spoke coolly to Nancy. Jacob Sidney was accompanied by a man he introduced as his legal adviser. All of them went to the third floor.

Interest centered upon Mr. Drew. He had taken his stand like a sentry at the door to the tower room and allowed no one to enter.

The two nephews pleaded for a chance to go into Asa Sidney's room "just to pick up a small keepsake," but were denied. When an opportunity came to speak to the lawyer privately, Jacob Sidney tried to learn what was in his great-uncle's will.

"I am not free to say at this time," Mr. Drew answered.

Midmorning a deputy from the sheriff's office arrived in response to the attorney's summons. He affixed a seal to the door of the tower room, where Asa Sidney had told Mr. Drew he kept valuable papers.

Mr. Drew's only response to all questions was, "I must comply with the law and the ethics of my profession."

He did, however, have a longer conversation with the Jemitts. "You are responsible for that room," he told them. "If the seal is broken you will be arrested. The windows are also locked and sealed so there is an additional responsibility to see that no one climbs in through them." Awestruck, the caretaker and his wife agreed to follow his orders.

At last Mr. Drew called the relatives together in the living room and told them of the funeral plans. "We'll meet here in two days to read the will," he added. "At two in the afternoon."

"If that's the earliest, all right," Peter Boonton assented with a grumble and the relatives left.

A little while later Mr. Drew took his daughter's car and drove off. Nancy went to talk to Carol, who was in her room. The girl was heartbroken.

"I feel so lonely," she confessed. "I hope Mr. Sidney left this house to the Jemitts. It's the only home I know, and it's full of memories of his kindness to me. I'd like to remain here—where I can see you often, Nancy."

"Don't worry, Carol. And for the next few days I'm going to stay with you all the time. Our darling housekeeper, Hannah Gruen, is coming out to be with us."

"Oh, thank you," Carol said. "That makes me feel so much better."

Mrs. Gruen arrived by taxi at lunchtime and the girls went down to meet her. She carried two suitcases, one of them Nancy's.

After expressing her sympathy to Carol, she asked, "What was being sent from this mansion in a truck?"

When Nancy and Carol said that they didn't know, Hannah went on, "There were several cartons. Here comes the man now who helped load them." Jemitt was striding toward the group from the kitchen.

"Hannah, this is Mr. Jemitt," Nancy introduced him. "I'd like—"

"This place is closed," he said abruptly. "Didn't you see the sign? No meals, no rooms."

Mrs. Gruen said with dignity, "I have been invited to stay here."

"By whom?" When Jemitt was told, he sneered, "Well, don't expect my wife and me to wait on you."

As he started to leave, Nancy said, "What were you sending from here in cartons?"

"What do you mean?"

Nancy explained and Jemitt answered, "Just some personal things. Your father told me and my wife to get out of here, so I've started packing." He hurried off.

"Hm!" said Mrs. Gruen. "I guess I've moved into a hornet's nest."

Nancy nodded in agreement, then whispered, "I wish I had my car here. I'd follow that truck."

"You can do it, anyway," Hannah Gruen told her. "Mose Blaine drove me here in his taxi. I had him wait in case you wanted to pick up your car. It's at your father's office."

"Oh you dear!" Nancy cried. She grabbed her purse, rushed from the inn, and jumped into the taxi. "Did you notice which direction that truck took?" she asked the driver.

"Yes. It went east."

"Please follow it," Nancy directed.

Mose Blaine looked surprised but did as she requested. Nancy said, "Don't break the law, but go as fast as you can."

The man grinned. "This buggy's kind o' old,

Miss Drew, and it's got rattles and creaks. I always say it groans with machinery rheumatiz pains."

Nancy smiled as she bounced and swayed on the rear seat. The taxi did not catch up to the truck until it pulled into the yard of a storage warehouse. Nancy asked Mose to wait for her at the curb. She waited until the driver of the truck went into the warehouse, then stepped out and walked into the yard. Pretending to give the cartons a casual glance, she looked for markings. One box lay on its side. Bold crayoned words read:

> FRANK JEMITT
>
> VALUABLE
>
> SPECIAL STORAGE

Were the contents of the cartons the property of Asa Sidney? Nancy wondered as she hurried back to the taxi. She directed Mose to Mr. Drew's office. When she reached it, Nancy paid the amount on the meter, gave the driver a generous tip, and stepped out.

He thanked her, then said, "Ain't you goin' to tell me what the mystery is?"

Nancy chuckled. "Someday, maybe." She headed for the office building.

Mr. Drew was amazed at her story and remarked, "You're on the job all right. When you arrive back at the inn with your own car, I doubt that Jemitt will suspect you followed the truck—and that's just as well."

As soon as Nancy returned to the Sidney mansion, she had lunch, then arranged with Mrs. Gruen and Carol to work subtly on one of two aspects of the case: they were to watch every movement of the Jemitts. She herself would continue to look for hidden articles.

The afternoon and evening wore on with no unusual happenings and no luck in her search. Hannah Gruen helped with the preparation of meals and tidied the house. In this way she was able to keep track of Mrs. Jemitt, while her husband's comings and goings were watched by Carol.

Nancy had found no more signs of a twisted candle, indicating hidden treasure. In her bedroom she made a discovery. Under the large rug a section of flooring was removable and Nancy pulled it up. To her disappointment, the space below was empty. Had the Jemitts removed something from the hiding place? she wondered.

Several times that day and the next Nancy found Carol alone, weeping. "I feel so terrible," she finally said. "My dear, true friend Mr. Sidney is gone. Now I'll have to leave this place with the Jemitts. Nancy, I just dread it."

Nancy comforted the girl the best she could, but had to admit that the outlook was bleak.

At last the funeral was over and the relatives gathered at The Sign of the Twisted Candles for the reading of the will. They assembled in the living room. George and Bess were there. The cousins nodded a solemn greeting to Nancy but stayed close to their parents.

Mr. Drew directed the Jemitts, Carol, and Nancy to be present. Nancy stood behind Carol, who had taken a seat at the edge of the circle of whispering relatives, her eyes downcast in shyness.

"We have met," Mr. Drew began, "to read the last will and testament of Mr. Asa Sidney. The document was written only a few days ago, in his own hand and in duplicate. The original is already filed in the courthouse. I hold the copy here. The two have been carefully compared and found to be exact duplicates.

"The will was witnessed by Mr. Raymond Hill, executive vice president of the Smith's Ferry branch of the River Heights National Bank. I preface the reading of these papers with these remarks because some of its provisions may surprise you. I may add that—although I am named sole executor of the estate—I had never met Mr. Sidney until I was summoned by him to help draw up this document."

Mr. Drew opened a bulky envelope, and unfolded some crisp sheets of paper.

"Mr. Hill, will you identify this testament?"

The banker, who had been seated unnoticed in one corner, arose, examined the papers, and nodded.

"That is my signature," he said. "And those are

my initials on each sheet. This is the document which Mr. Sidney prepared, and which I witnessed." He sat down.

"Hurry up with the reading and cut out the fancy business!" Jacob Sidney called out.

Mr. Drew shot him a disapproving look. Then he began to read, while everyone except Carol leaned forward tensely.

" 'I, Asa Sidney, being of sound mind, although in the hundred and first year of my life, do hereby declare this to be my last will and testament, prepared by my own hand, legally witnessed, and replaces all previous wills made by me.

" 'First, all my just debts are to be paid. Following that, all my property, real and personal, is to be disposed of after my death, as follows:

" ' "These relatives of myself and my wife, namely Jacob Sidney, Peter Boonton, Anna Boonton Marvin and her daughter Bess Marvin, Louise Boonton Fayne and her daughter George Fayne, as well as the young woman known as Carol Wipple, shall select by mutual consent and in the order named one article of furniture from my belongings as a permanent keepsake.' "

"Oh, Nancy, he didn't forget me!" Carol whispered.

" 'Excepting,' " Mr. Drew continued with emphasis, " 'the portrait of my late, beloved wife, which will be disposed of hereinafter.

" 'I then direct that all my other property be

converted into cash by legal sale at the best current price as soon as possible after my death.' "

There followed a list of items to be sold. The house, with four hundred acres of surrounding land, headed the list. Then came a piece of valuable real estate in the heart of the River Heights business district. Two bank accounts and a quantity of stocks and bonds were mentioned.

Mr. Drew read on, " 'The bankbooks, deeds, receipts, and some of the securities are in a black wooden chest bound in brass on the lid of which is my name.' "

Nancy glanced at her father. How glad she was that she had rescued it!

" 'I further direct,' " the will stated, "that the money realized from these shall be divided into nine equal parts.' "

At this, all the relatives sat up straight, and calculating looks were exchanged among the possible heirs.

" 'One share shall again be divided into seven equal parts,' " Mr. Drew continued solemnly, and the now-bewildered relatives sat further forward on their chairs. " 'One of these shares, that is, one sixty-third of the entire estate, shall be given to Frank Jemitt and his wife Emma in consideration of those days a few years ago during which they served me honestly and well.' "

For a moment all eyes turned to the couple. So Asa Sidney did suspect them of recent thefts!

" 'One each of the remaining sub-shares, namely one sixty-third of the entire estate, shall be given to each of my relatives, namely Jacob Sidney, Peter Boonton, Anna Marvin, Bess Marvin, Louise Fayne, and George Fayne.

" 'All the rest of the money, to wit, eight-ninths of the cash proceeds of the estate, shall be given to the girl known as Carol Wipple, who shall also inherit the portrait of my wife—' "

A concerted growl of disapproval arose from the disappointed heirs as Nancy cried out in alarm:

"Carol has fainted!"

CHAPTER XII

The Mysterious Attic

"Get a glass of water!" Raymond Hill called to Frank Jemitt, who did not look as angered and disappointed as Asa Sidney's relatives.

Jemitt hurried to the kitchen and returned with a tumbler of water. Nancy moistened a handkerchief and laid it on Carol's forehead. Then she massaged the back of her neck and wrists.

Carol stirred and sat up. "I—I must have fainted," she murmured. "Oh, Nancy, there you are. Please don't go away."

No one else offered to help; they sat still and waited. But finally Jacob Sidney exclaimed, "We'll fight this out in court!"

"You bet we will," Peter Boonton seconded. "There isn't a court in the world that will uphold this will. Asa Sidney couldn't have been in his right mind when he cheated his own relatives and left most of his estate to a stranger!"

Mr. Drew made no reply to the threats. Instead, he went on reading.

" 'I direct my sole executor, Carson Drew, to have the Fernwood Orphanage review Carol Wipple's case, and if in their judgment they find Frank and Emma Jemitt unfit to continue as her foster parents, that it assign new foster parents to her.' "

"Oh!" Carol cried out. For a second, Nancy thought she was going to faint again.

"That's ridiculous!" Frank Jemitt burst out. "We've always been kind and gentle to Carol and given her a good home."

"We sure have," his wife added. "Why, Carol, you wouldn't think of letting anyone take you from us, would you?"

Nancy was disgusted by this sudden attitude of pretended affection and hoped Carol would not be influenced by it.

Mr. Drew had not finished. After completing the reading of the will, he said, "Mr. Asa Sidney told me that he had a special reason for remembering Carol in his will. At the time he was too tired to tell me about it but promised to give me the whole story later. Unfortunately he never had a chance."

Everyone looked at Carol, and Jacob Sidney shouted, "What did he mean?"

"I—I don't know," Carol faltered. "He was kind to me and I did what I could for him."

The relatives arose in a body, ignored the girl, barely nodded to the others in the room and left the old mansion. Nancy was incensed by their attitude and deeply hurt by the actions of Bess and George.

As soon as they had gone, and Mr. Drew had walked into the hall with Mr. Hill, Nancy said to Carol, "This has been a hard day for you. Why don't you go up to your room and lie down?"

"Oh, Nancy, I'd only think more if I did that."

"Of course you would," Mrs. Jemitt spoke up. "What you need is a mother's tender loving care. Come with me."

"No, no!" Carol objected, clinging to Nancy.

The Jemitts went off. Hannah Gruen appeared and urged Carol and Nancy to have some tea and toast in the kitchen.

"All right," Carol agreed. "And I'll tell you about the will, Mrs. Gruen. Oh, I suppose I'll be rich but it scares me."

Nancy said good-by to her father and Mr. Hill, then joined Carol and Hannah. After the men had driven off, she began to wonder where the Jemitts were.

"I think I'll prowl around a bit," she told the others.

Nancy went quietly to the second floor. Seeing no one, she continued to the tower room. Frank Jemitt was crouched at the door, studying the official padlock placed there by the sheriff. The flashlight in his hand cast flickering shadows on the white walls.

"Oh, there you are, Mr. Jemitt," Nancy said pleasantly.

The startled man wheeled on his heels. "I—I was just making sure none of the relatives had sneaked up here to burglarize the place," he stammered.

"And did you find everything secure?"

"Oh yes," he growled, and rushed down the stairs past the girl.

Nancy followed Jemitt to the second floor and saw him enter his bedroom. She went into her own room but left the door ajar. A few minutes later he came out with Mrs. Jemitt. The couple hurried to the first floor and out the front door.

Nancy returned to Carol and Hannah, and suggested that the two girls stroll around the grounds. The back lawn was weedy and littered, and the ramshackle old barn gave the garden a shabby appearance.

A flicker of light inside the barn aroused Nancy's suspicions. Taking Carol by the hand, she led her into the nearby woods.

"Let's watch the barn from here," she said, "where we won't be noticed. I want to see if Jemitt brings anything outside."

At that instant Jemitt stepped from the building and surveyed the house and yard. Then he ducked back inside. Presently he emerged with two long boxes which he carried with difficulty.

"He's going away from the road," Nancy muttered. "What's at the rear of the property, Carol?"

"Just pastures and meadows and the old tenant farmer's house," Carol whispered.

"We'll follow Jemitt," Nancy decided. "Can we get to that house without leaving the woods?"

"There's a roundabout way," Carol said. "I'll show you."

Stepping carefully so as not to cause any sound, the two girls made their way among the trees. Soon Jemitt was out of sight, but still Nancy urged Carol on, convinced that the deserted tenant house was the man's goal. After ten minutes of difficult going, Carol stopped and pointed.

"There's the old tenant house," she said. "And, Nancy, you uncanny mind reader, my foster father's just leaving it!"

"And without the boxes!" Nancy added. "We'll wait until he's gone and then search the place."

The building smelled musty and dirty. Inside, the light from the setting sun shone dimly through cobwebby, dusty windows. The floor was thick with debris and fallen plaster.

"See these footprints. They go directly upstairs," Nancy remarked.

The two girls crept up the creaking, wobbly old steps, their hearts thumping with excitement. The second floor was merely an unplastered attic. A rusted iron bed stood under the eaves, and an antique wardrobe, its doors awry and its once fine mahogany surface green with mildew, leaned against the chimney.

Nancy looked into the huge piece of furniture. "All the shelves have been taken away!" she observed. "The wardrobe's empty."

Nancy turned to examine the floor. She became interested in part of a plank that had less litter on it than the others.

"It's getting late," Carol murmured nervously.

"We'll go in a minute," Nancy said.

She knelt and with her slim fingertips drew the loose nails from the wide floorboard and pulled it up.

Carol gasped! Four boxes were revealed, two of them obviously the ones Jemitt had just brought. Nancy stooped to throw back the lid of one when a step creaked on the stairway. Someone was coming!

"It must be Father Jemitt!" Carol chattered, clutching at Nancy.

"This way, quick!" Nancy said.

She pushed Carol into the moldering old wardrobe, crowded in beside her, and pulled the doors as nearly shut as possible. The stairs continued to creak as someone slowly mounted them. Carol gripped Nancy's arm, trembling violently. A shadowy figure appeared at the head of the steps and paused to survey the attic.

"That isn't Father Jemitt," Carol whispered. "This man's too tall."

"Sh!" Nancy warned.

He entered the attic and gave a start upon seeing the displaced floorboard. The newcomer stooped to look into the opening, and evidently lifted the lids of the boxes.

Then he straightened up and scanned the entire room. As his face was revealed in the dim light, Nancy almost gave a startled exclamation. The man was Raymond Hill, the banker from Smith's Ferry!

What was he doing here? Had he betrayed Carson Drew's trust and confidence? Had the lure of old Asa's fortune overcome his scruples, too? Nancy was tense as these questions raced through her mind.

Meanwhile, Mr. Hill paced slowly around the attic. Nancy was certain he would eventually pull open the doors of the antique wardrobe and find the two girls.

A plank creaked under Mr. Hill's feet and he stopped, bent down, and gave a little chuckle. Nancy saw him pry the nails loose and lift the board. He reached into the opening and pulled out a metal box used for filing valuable documents.

Mr. Hill opened it and took a bundle of papers from it. Nancy guessed they were stock certificates. He looked through them, stuffed the bundle into his pocket, and replaced the loose flooring, after kicking the box out of sight.

Now Mr. Hill's eyes roved about the attic and at last fastened on the old wardrobe. He began to walk toward it slowly, testing the planks beneath his feet at every step.

Nancy was thinking fast. Should she emerge from her hiding place or gamble that Mr. Hill would not open the wardrobe?

A sinister sight interrupted her thoughts. Standing at the head of the steps, up which he had crept with practiced caution, was Frank Jemitt! His eyes gleamed unbelievingly as he watched Mr. Hill's movements closely.

At that moment the banker glanced about the attic once more. Nancy saw him stiffen when he detected the other man.

"Mr. Jemitt!" the banker said, unruffled. "What are you bringing up here now to hide? Come, let me see it!"

Jemitt mounted the top step and strode toward Mr. Hill. In his arms was something tightly wrapped in newspapers.

"I don't know why you're here trespassing," Jemitt snarled. "But if you want to see what I have, here it is!"

To Nancy's horror, he hurled his burden full force at Mr. Hill. The paper fell off, revealing a square metal box. The banker ducked but a corner of the box caught his shoulder, causing him to lose his balance and almost fall.

That was the advantage Jemitt wanted. He rushed forward with flailing fists. Mr. Hill threw up his arms to protect his face. Jemitt thrust out a foot and sent the tall man sprawling onto his back.

In a flash Jemitt was on top of him. One hand gripped Mr. Hill's throat, while the other pounded his face and head.

"You coward!" Nancy exclaimed, and burst from the wardrobe. "Stop that!"

She flew at Jemitt and seized his shirt collar at the back with both hands to drag him away.

CHAPTER XIII

Fleeing Suspects

"Who's that? What are—?" Jemitt choked.

He craned his neck, and when he saw that Nancy was his new opponent he bared his teeth and snarled, "Let go of me, or I'll do worse than this to you."

Nancy's response was to twist her fingers deeper into the man's collar and tug harder. Realizing that he had an unexpected ally, Mr. Hill squirmed free of Jemitt's grasp and drove his fist deep into the innkeeper's stomach.

The man doubled over with a gasp, the breath knocked out of him. Mr. Hill arose, his clothing dirty and rumpled, his face rapidly swelling with bruises.

"Why, Nancy! And Carol! How did you get here?" the banker gasped.

"We were here first," Nancy said. "We heard

you coming, and not knowing who it was we hid in the wardrobe."

"You saved me from this madman!" Mr. Hill said. "Say, did *you* pull up that loose plank over there?"

"Yes," Nancy replied. "We were just going to look in the boxes when you frightened us off."

Mr. Hill shook his head and smiled weakly. "Nancy, your father sent me back to help you hunt for more of Asa Sidney's fortune, but it was you who saved the day for me! I saw Jemitt coming from this house and traced his path to find out what he was up to—and you know the rest!" Nancy chided herself for her earlier suspicions of Raymond Hill's integrity.

Jemitt, clutching his middle, rose shakily to his feet. "Carol," he said, "shall I call the police and have this man arrested for trespassing?"

"Arrest me?" the banker shouted.

"Arrest Mr. Hill? Why?" Carol and Nancy gasped in unison.

"For trying to steal old man Sidney's valuables, of course," Jemitt replied. "Why else do you think he was poking around here where Mr. Sidney used to hide his things?"

"Of all the false statements!" the banker bellowed. "You're the thief!"

"Ha-ha! Deny if you can that you took a bunch of bonds from under the floor and have them in your pocket this minute!" Jemitt challenged.

"I don't deny it, and here they are," Mr. Hill declared, disclosing the securities. "I didn't steal them. Whoever hid them there stole them."

"Tell that to the judge!" the innkeeper jeered. "Old Asa hid them there himself! Come along, Carol. Both these smart crooks are trying to rob you of your inheritance. I'll drive you to town and ask for a detective to guard you. And we'll hunt up a lawyer without a smarty daughter."

"No, I don't want to be with you again," Carol cried. "Go away, please, and stay away!"

"You'll be sorry someday you said that." Jemitt gave a forced laugh. "When these new friends of yours have stripped you of everything you own, you'll come around begging Frank and Emma to be good to you again."

Nancy looked sternly at Jemitt. "How about that ebony box with brass bindings that you buried under a woodpile?" she asked. "It might mean that any visits you'll have from Carol will be in the state penitentiary!"

Jemitt opened his mouth as if to retort, but instead turned and walked down the dark stairs.

"We must find out where he's going!" Nancy said, stooping to pick up the box Jemitt had hurled at Mr. Hill. "And I'll call my Dad and report to him."

Mr. Hill took the box from Nancy, and suggested they should also remove the other boxes from under the floorboards. They lifted them out and started for the house.

"I'll give you a receipt for these and put them in the bank vault," he said to Nancy. "They certainly aren't safe here."

"But the bank isn't open," Nancy told him.

"It will be until seven this evening."

Mr. Hill and the girls trailed Jemitt across the meadow to the Sidney mansion. When they arrived, Hannah said he and his wife had gone to their room.

Nancy nodded. "I'll phone Dad and tell him what happened."

"Then I'll call my chauffeur," Mr. Hill told her.

She ran to the telephone booth and called her home. No one answered, so Nancy tried her father's office. His secretary was still there and explained she was working late.

"Mr. Drew went out of town in connection with the Sidney case, and won't be back until tomorrow afternoon," she said. "That's why he sent Mr. Hill out to see if you were all right."

"Thank you," said Nancy. "We're having an exciting time but we're all okay."

Mr. Hill made his call and in a short time was ready to leave. "I think," he said, "that I'd better come back here tonight and keep an eye on things."

Nancy smiled. "Oh, would you? We'll have dinner ready by that time."

Carol insisted upon helping. Mrs. Gruen remarked that the Jemitts also should be offering to do their share.

"They'll get hungry some time," the Drews' housekeeper said. "Then we'll see them."

Nancy had chosen to set the table in the dining room so she could watch the couple come downstairs. But half an hour went by and they did not appear. Uneasy, Nancy decided to go upstairs and speak to them. She found their door wide open and the closet stripped of clothes. On a hunch Nancy pulled out several bureau drawers. There was nothing in them!

"They've gone!" she thought in dismay. "No telling what they took with them!"

Nancy fairly flew to the first floor and burst into the kitchen. "The Jemitts have moved out!" she exclaimed.

"What!" said Hannah Gruen. "But how could they without our seeing them?"

Carol sank into a chair. "It's all my fault. I've made such a mess of everything!" she wailed. "Th-the Jemitts must have used the back stairway."

She explained that since several steps on it needed repairing, the stairway was never used. At the top and bottom, planks had been laid across and curtains hung at the back. The spaces were used as closets.

"Please show me," Nancy requested.

She and Hannah followed the girl to a rear hall which opened onto a porch. Carol grasped the handle of an inside door and turned it. A curtain three feet beyond had been shoved aside, revealing a stairway. There was no doubt but that the Jemitts had used it in their secret getaway.

"I wonder how much of Asa Sidney's property they took," Mrs. Gruen remarked grimly.

Carol shuddered at the remark. "You really think they have stolen *more* of Mr. Sidney's possessions?"

Nancy nodded. "It's a good possibility." A determined look spread over her face. "I'm going to find those people!"

Hannah smiled. "I'm sure nobody wants them back, but as foster parents they did abandon a minor, and are liable."

"Carol, is there a big flashlight around?" Nancy asked.

"Yes, in the kitchen."

"We'll need it. Carol, you help me. Hannah, please guard the house," Nancy directed.

The two girls rushed outside just in time to meet Mr. Hill walking in. His chauffeur was driving off. Quickly Nancy explained what had happened and the three rushed to the garage. As they had expected, the Jemitts' car was gone.

"We didn't hear the motor," Nancy said, "so it's my guess the Jemitts pushed the car out to the road before starting it. Let's take mine and try to catch them!"

She had parked her convertible in the driveway, near the far corner of the inn. When they reached the car, all of them gasped in dismay. Both rear tires had been slashed.

"How awful!" Carol exclaimed.

"And I have only one spare tire," Nancy said, vexed with herself because the Jemitts had outwitted her. An idea came to her. "The tire-cutting was probably done to prevent pursuit," she said. "Or maybe the Jemitts wanted to make us believe pursuit is necessary, but actually they're not far away!"

She turned to Mr. Hill. "What was in the boxes you took to the bank besides the securities?"

"A large collection of sterling silver," he replied. "I'm sure that old tenant house is filled with loot."

"Then that's where the Jemitts would go first," Nancy said with conviction. She took a large portable spotlight from her car trunk. "Let's hurry to the tenant house," she urged.

The three strode off through the meadows to the old cottage. Nancy was somewhat disappointed to find it in darkness.

"They got here ahead of us," Mr. Hill commented. "That is, if they came here at all."

"Let's wait a few minutes," Nancy said, putting out the light.

They stood in silence close to a towering syca-more tree, their forms blending with the light, mottled background of the trunk. At last Nancy's keen ears heard a sound that was different from the noises of the meadow insects. It had a metallic ring and was muffled and distant.

Instantly she switched on her spotlight, and the beam cut through the blackness. The tumble-down tenant house sprang into view, and on the rickety front steps Frank and Emma Jemitt were etched sharply in the glare. He was carrying a long, narrow box over one shoulder. His wife held a pair of ornate silver candelabra.

"Call to them that the house is guarded and that they must leave anything they have re-moved," Nancy whispered to Mr. Hill. "Try to disguise your voice."

Raymond Hill chuckled, cleared his throat, and then in a resounding voice shouted the warning Nancy had requested.

"Who are you, anyhow?" Jemitt yelled back. "I got a right to be here!"

"Stand where you are!" Mr. Hill commanded.

Jemitt gave an ugly laugh in response and moved a step lower.

"If we could frighten them," whispered Nancy, "with a loud noise, such as—"

"Um—yes."

Nancy picked up a stone. "I wonder—"

Mr. Hill quickly sensed her thought, grabbed

the rock, then with a fling sent it toward the cottage at a swift pace. There was the crash of glass as a front window shattered into splinters.

Jemitt picked up the box, leaped off the steps, and ran into the darkness. Mrs. Jemitt screamed and dashed after her husband. Nancy kept the spotlight on the panic-stricken pair as they charged through the brush and meadow grass toward the road.

"We must stop them and see what's in their car!" Nancy exclaimed.

She led the others, but the chase proved hopeless. Halfway up the road they heard the roar of a motor and a car speed off.

"I think," said Mr. Hill as the three retraced their steps, "that as soon as dinner is over, I'd better come back to the tenant house and guard it. In fact, this would give me a chance to do some more searching."

Carol shyly offered an army cot and blankets from the inn.

"I accept," the banker said. "And I'll take a flashlight too."

After finishing the delicious dinner Hannah had prepared, Mr. Hill left. Nancy could not get her mind off the Jemitts and finally phoned her friend Police Chief McGinnis in River Heights and told him the story.

"I'm glad you called me," the officer said. "This is serious. My men will be alerted to watch for the

"We must stop them!" Nancy exclaimed

Jemitts. If they're located, the car will be searched. The sign of the twisted candles on anything they find will identify it as Asa Sidney's property."

Mrs. Gruen had already insisted that the exhausted and weepy Carol go to bed. When Nancy went up to say good night to her, the girl was sound asleep.

Nancy returned to the first floor just in time to answer the telephone. A male voice asked, "Is Miss Nancy Drew there?"

The young detective's face broke into a wide smile. "Hi, Ned!" she exclaimed.

"For Pete's sake, Nancy, I've been trying for days to get you. What's the idea of hiding?"

"Oh, Ned, I have so much to tell you. When can you leave your job and come down so I can talk to you?"

"Camp closes tomorrow. I should be home the next day. By the way, what's up between you and Bess? When I couldn't get your house I called her to find out where you were. Boy, she was about as friendly as an ice cube!"

"I'll tell you when I see you," Nancy answered. "You'd better call me again before you leave, Ned. I may go home."

"Okay. Be good. By now."

"By."

After the dinner dishes had been washed and put away, Nancy and Hannah Gruen sat down in the living room to talk. The conversation turned to possible treasures hidden in the house.

"One place old-timers always hid things was in chimneys," the Drews' housekeeper remarked.

"There are several in this house," Nancy said. Jumping up, she added, "Let's investigate the one in here first."

Nancy brought her flashlight and looked up inside the chimney. She could see nothing because the damper was closed. Noting a hook, Nancy gave it a yank. The next moment a shower of black soot and debris sprayed down over her.

Hannah Gruen gasped. Then the next second she cried out, "Ugh! Bats!"

CHAPTER XIV

An Embarrassing Meeting

AFRAID to open her eyes Nancy stepped from the fireplace and felt for a handkerchief from her pocket. Hannah kept crying, "Bats! Bats! Look out, Nancy! They may bite you!"

Nancy could hardly see but realized that two bats were whizzing around the room. Apparently they were confused by their sudden exit into the lighted room from the dark chimney. Mrs. Gruen, who had flipped the back of her skirt over her head, was rushing to the front door, which she flung open.

"Get out! Shoo!" she cried out.

By now Nancy had wiped the soot from her eyes and joined Hannah in trying to force the bats from the house. Finally the housekeeper ran outside. Nancy followed and in a minute the flying mammals came too. Nancy and Hannah hurried back inside.

"Thank goodness they've gone!" Hannah said. "And now, Nancy, you'd better go upstairs for a bath and a shampoo while I clean up that mess in the living room."

Nancy needed no urging. She shook off as much soot as possible, then went upstairs. At last, too weary for further treasure hunting, she went to bed.

Carol was both alarmed and amused by Nancy's story of the bats the next morning, and for the first time in days a smile came over her pale face. "I can just see you standing there, black from head to foot."

Nancy laughed. "I'll confine my hunting to cleaner spots."

As the girls helped Mrs. Gruen prepare breakfast, they saw Mr. Hill striding toward the house.

"Good morning!" the banker hailed them. "All quiet at the tenant house last night. Any excitement here?"

"Plenty," Nancy replied, and told him about the chimney episode. He laughed heartily.

Soon the four were enjoying a hearty breakfast.

"I'll have to go to the bank," Mr. Hill said presently. "My chauffeur will call for me, and then I'll send him back to stand guard at the tenant house."

"We'll stay here in the inn," Nancy told him. "As soon as my father returns I'll ask him to station two watchmen here, one to relieve your chauffeur. Then Mrs. Gruen and I will go home and take Carol with us."

"An excellent plan—the best possible under the circumstances," Mr. Hill declared. "Nancy, you certainly won a major battle of wits against the Jemitts at the tenant house last night."

The banker's car arrived shortly, and he rode off. In less than an hour the chauffeur was back with new tires for Nancy's car. He deftly put them on before taking up guard duty at the old cottage.

At noontime Nancy telephoned her father's office and learned that he had just returned. Swiftly she outlined the events of the preceding day, and he promised that precautions such as Nancy suggested would be taken. At one o'clock an automobile drove up. In it with Mr. Drew were two muscular men.

"Private detectives," the lawyer said briefly to Nancy.

He posted one man at the inn, the other at the tenant house. The guards were to be replaced by another duo at midnight.

"Now, Carol, pack your things and we'll take off," Nancy said. "Our worries are over for the time being."

While Carol was packing, Mr. Drew told Nancy that the Sidney-Boonton families had engaged a lawyer to fight Carol's inheritance from Asa Sidney.

"That's a contest where I can't help you, can

I?" Nancy asked. "I wish I were old enough to be a lawyer!"

"You've already done a fine job," her father said. "And I'm sure we'll win the lawsuit. It would help very much, though, if we had some supportable testimony as to why Mr. Sidney favored this orphan girl above his entire family."

They stopped speaking as Carol came down the stairway wearing a shabby coat and carrying an old-fashioned suitcase. She apologized for both. "I never went anywhere, and wore uniforms most of the time, so I didn't need any clothes."

This gave Nancy an idea. "Carol," she said, "you deserve a good-looking wardrobe. Let's go downtown on a shopping spree! I have charge accounts, and you can pay me back when you receive allowances from your inheritance. We'll buy dresses and shoes, and a coat, and—"

"Oh, I can't believe it!" Carol exclaimed. "This could be the biggest thrill of my life!"

"It'll be a lot of fun for me, too," Nancy declared as she locked the front door and gave the key to the watchman. "Let's go now."

She took Hannah home first, then set off for the shopping center of River Heights. As Nancy led Carol into the elevator of a big department store, she discovered that the only other occupants were Bess and George!

The two cousins smiled timidly at the other

girls. Then, as if remembering that they were told not to be friendly, they turned aside.

Impulsively Nancy put her hand on Bess's arm. "Bess," she said softly, "I've done nothing. Why must our friendship be broken because of a foolish quarrel that persons now dead had seventy years ago?"

To Nancy's surprise a big tear rolled down Bess's cheek. George bit her lip nervously, glancing from Bess to Nancy.

"We can't help it, Nancy," she said finally. "Your father is responsible for keeping our family from its rightful share in Asa Sidney's estate."

"Oh no!" Nancy said. "Lets talk this over," she suggested. "In the tearoom."

Hesitatingly the cousins agreed, and soon the four girls were seated in a quiet corner of the store's restaurant.

"Bess, you and George met Carol the same evening I did," Nancy began. "It was the first time we three had seen Mr. Sidney."

Bess and George nodded, and Nancy continued, "I mentioned that my father was a lawyer and that night Carol phoned me and said Mr. Sidney wanted to make a new will and would Dad come to draw it the next morning. Mr. Sidney seemed perfectly competent to me. He didn't appear to you to be unbalanced, did he?"

Bess and George looked at each other uncomfortably, then shook their heads.

"It's my father's duty to carry out his client's wishes," Nancy went on. "Well, that's my story. Carol's is just as simple. Mr. Sidney chose to make her one of his heirs. It hasn't brought her happiness because of the way your family and the others are treating her."

"That's true," Carol said.

"The family feud should not interfere with our friendship," Nancy went on. "Why let the anger of great-uncles come between us?"

"Nancy," George declared, "you're absolutely right. I'm sorry and ashamed of the way I've acted. Please forgive me. I want to be friends."

"Oh, Nancy," Bess cried, "I'm so glad we're talking to one another again. And, Carol, I'm not going to do anything to break the will."

"I'm not either," George added quickly.

Nancy laughed in relief and the others joined in.

"What are you girls shopping for?" George asked. "We always have so much fun buying things with Nancy."

"Carol wants to get some new clothes," Nancy explained. "Want to help?"

"You bet!" Bess and George answered.

When the store closed that evening, the four girls left it chatting merrily and laden with bundles. Carol had been outfitted from head to toe in attractive clothes. Her hair had been trimmed and modishly combed at the beauty salon. She looked very lovely and seemed to have gained self-confidence.

But she was not yet entirely at ease. On the way home, she whispered to Nancy, "Please don't go far from me. I'm so afraid the Jemitts may try to harm me. Nancy, do you mind if I don't go back yet to the old mansion to hunt for the hidden treasures?"

"Of course not, Carol. I think you'll be happier at my house with Mrs. Gruen. Just take it easy, and don't worry."

Mr. Drew reached home at six o'clock and soon everyone sat down to dinner. Conversation was general, but as soon as the meal was over, he asked his daughter to follow him into his study. He closed the door and they sat down.

"Nancy," he said, "I have a lot to tell you. There's no use upsetting Carol. That's why I wanted to talk to you alone. A theory has been forming in my mind."

"About Carol's background?"

"Yes."

"You suspect Asa Sidney knew who she was?"

The lawyer nodded. "I made a trip to the Fernwood Orphanage and looked at all the old records. There was not a clue as to who Carol's parents might have been. But I did pick up some other interesting facts."

Mr. Drew said that Asa Sidney had been a trustee of the orphanage for many years. He had taken a great fancy to a certain little girl who had been given the name Sadie Wipple and he insisted it be changed to Carol. The name of the child he had lost was Carol.

"Then when the Jemitts, who owned a small restaurant, offered to become foster parents, Mr. Sidney would not give his consent unless the Jemitts agreed to come to his home and work. Frank and Emma did not want to be servants, so the arrangement about the tearoom and the promise of a share in Asa's will was worked out."

Nancy was intrigued by this information. "Dad, do you think that if Mr. Sidney had lived he would have told you everything?"

"I believe so. Now, unfortunately, we'll have to unearth the secret ourselves. And if we don't, I'm afraid those grasping relatives will take the case to court."

"Two of the heirs aren't going to join in," Nancy said with a chuckle, and told about being on friendly terms again with Bess and George.

"Well, my congratulations," her father said. "I wish your influence could extend to their parents and great-uncles. By the way, my main reason for going to the Fernwood Orphanage was to tell the directors of the request in Asa Sidney's will that the Jemitts be investigated and probably new foster parents be obtained for Carol."

"But now the Jemitts have run away," Nancy reminded her father.

"That in itself will be enough to take Carol away from them," the lawyer said. "I'll phone the orphanage and ask permission to keep her here until they decide about new foster parents."

"I'm sure the Jemitts will be back," Nancy remarked. "Either to get things they've cached away, or to hunt for others."

"By the way," Mr. Drew said, "I was able to get a court order freezing the contents of those cartons Jemitt stored in the warehouse."

As he finished speaking, Nancy stiffened in her chair. She had just seen a menacing face at the partially opened window.

CHAPTER XV

Candles' Secrets

"What's the matter?" Mr. Drew asked, turning so he too could look out the window.

"I saw Frank Jemitt looking in!" Nancy exclaimed.

She and her father rushed outdoors to accost the man, but could not find him. Mr. Drew was worried that Jemitt had overheard the conversation between Nancy and himself and might use it to his own advantage.

"How?" Nancy asked.

"By conniving with the relatives and threatening Carol."

To avoid similar incidents in the future, Mr. Drew requested that all the windows in the house be closed and locked, and the air-conditioning system turned on.

"I don't think," said Nancy, "we should worry Carol with all this." Her father agreed.

Their guest slept well. As soon as she came

downstairs, Carol insisted upon being given some household chores. "I'm so used to work I wouldn't know what to do with myself."

Mr. Drew smiled at her. "I suggest that you help Mrs. Gruen and in between jobs do a lot of reading. By the way, Carol, you want to go back to school, don't you?"

"Oh yes."

"I think," the lawyer went on, "that we should look for a good boarding school for you. Of course the orphanage and your new foster parents will have to decide which one."

Carol was silent for several seconds. Then she said, "I suppose so. But I'll hate leaving the nice new friends I've made." She looked wistfully at Nancy, who smiled encouragingly.

"You can visit us."

The telephone rang. Nancy answered it. "Oh hi, Ned!"

He asked if she would be free for lunch. "I'd like to take you out and maybe you could show me that mysterious old inn. How's the case progressing?"

"It's a long story. I'll tell you when I see you," she replied.

"See you at twelve."

Nancy explained to Carol that Ned was a student at Emerson College and they had been dating for some time. "Maybe I'll ask Bess and George to come over and keep you company."

Carol shook her head. "Nancy, I'd just like to be quiet, and—and bake a surprise for your dinner tonight."

"That would be great," Nancy said. "May I guess what it'll be?"

The other girl smiled. "I'll tell you the name but you'll never guess what it is. Ever hear of Butterfly Pie?"

"No." Nancy laughed. "Sounds alive. I'll look forward to it."

Ned arrived promptly and drove Nancy to a country restaurant. Tables surrounded a pool.

"How about a swim first?" he suggested. "We can rent some gear."

She agreed and they spent half an hour in the water. While they ate, Nancy brought Ned up to date on the mystery.

"Let's go to the inn and do some searching," he proposed.

"All right. Any place except the tower room. It has been sealed by the sheriff's office. The watchman has keys to the house."

When they arrived at the mansion the guard greeted Nancy. She introduced Ned and said they would like to go in and look around.

"I'll let you in, but I sure had a bad time with those two other guys and that couple when I told 'em No."

"Who were they?" Nancy asked.

"I don't know." His description of them fitted

Jacob Sidney, Peter Boonton, and the Jemitts. "They all wanted to look in the tower room."

"Is the other guard still at the tenant house?" Nancy asked.

"Why no. Didn't you hear that your father dismissed him?"

Nancy was astounded. She had a strong hunch this was not true. As soon as the front door was opened, she dashed to the telephone to call Mr. Drew. To her dismay she found that the cord had been cut in half!

"Ned, come here!" she called.

He gazed at the severed cord critically. "Vandalism all right. Whom do you suspect?"

Nancy said she was sure Jemitt was responsible. "When the guard was around the corner, Jemitt let himself into the house. To avoid arrest if detected, he made it impossible for anyone to phone."

"What about the other guard?" Ned asked. "Do you think Jemitt faked a note to get rid of him?"

"Yes."

Ned suggested that they report the damage to the telephone company at once. "Let's drive to the nearest phone right now."

"You go," Nancy said. "I'd like to look around here."

Left alone, Nancy went from room to room. Nothing on the first floor seemed to have been disturbed. She figured that probably the Jemitts had already removed any visible expensive objects. She hurried to the second floor and peered into one room after another. When Nancy reached the room she had occupied, the young sleuth stopped short.

On the bed lay a man bound and gagged! His eyes were closed. Apparently he was asleep, because he did not move.

Nancy tiptoed over. He was Jacob Sidney! Quickly she pulled off the gag. The motion aroused the man, who seemed to be dazed. But finally his eyes fastened on the young detective.

"*You!*" he said in a hoarse whisper. "How did I get here?"

"I don't know. I just found you. What happened?"

"Untie me and I'll tell you."

Nancy did not trust Jacob Sidney. Why was he in this house that he was not supposed to enter? She would wait until Ned's return.

"First tell me how you got in here," Nancy said.

Grudgingly he admitted trying the door when the guard's back was turned. "I found it unlocked and slipped in. I thought I'd better come here and —and protect my inheritance," he added lamely. "Suddenly somebody hit me from the back and that's all I remember."

There was the sound of approaching footsteps. Ned walked in and Nancy signaled him not to act too startled.

Jacob Sidney, apparently mistaking Ned for a plainclothes police detective, said, "I had a right to be here, Officer. I've inherited part of this property."

As Ned leaned over and untied the man's bonds, Nancy said, "This is Mr. Jacob Sidney."

"Well, Mr. Sidney," Ned remarked, "I advise you to leave at once and not come back."

"I will, I will," the crestfallen intruder said.

He got up stiffly, went down the stairs, and out the front door. Not until he was outside did Nancy and Ned burst into laughter.

Ned remarked, "I guess that snoopy beneficiary won't be back in a hurry."

"Not with you around, Officer," said Nancy.

"I got your father," Ned reported. "He certainly didn't dismiss the guard, and is sending the man back. A repairman from the phone company will be here to replace the cord. Probably the person who cut the cord is responsible for the dismissal of the watchman and the knockout blow to Jacob Sidney."

"Let's see what other damage he may have caused," Nancy suggested.

They opened closet doors and Nancy even investigated the camouflaged back stairway, but found nothing suspicious. She showed Ned the hidden ornate music box before they began a hunt for other treasures.

"I'm to look for the sign of a twisted candle?" Ned asked.

"Uh-huh," she answered.

Every panel in the ceilings, walls, and floorboards was carefully examined. The couple became separated and there was not a sound for nearly half an hour.

Then Ned cried out, "Nancy! Come here! I think I've found something!"

She ran to his side in the rear hall. "Look! The grass cloth on this wall is a little different from the rest and a twisted candle has been carefully worked into the design. Do you think it means anything?"

Nancy ran her fingers over the rough fabric. "It's lumpy underneath!" she said excitedly. "Ned, we should investigate!"

For a moment Nancy wondered if they should tear off the wall covering. "It's old and faded, anyway," she told Ned.

He agreed. "We'll use my penknife and be as careful as possible," he said.

Inch by inch he felt the lumpy area and cut around it. Then he peeled off the grass cloth.

"A safe!" Nancy exclaimed.

"Right," said Ned. "And how are we going to find out the combination to it?" He grinned. "One thing I haven't learned is how to be a safe-cracker."

Nancy laughed, then reached up and tried the recessed knob. To her amazement it turned!

"Oh, Ned, the safe isn't locked!"

In a moment the door was open. The couple peered inside.

"Swords!" said Ned.

He lifted one out. It was encrusted with jewels and evidently very old and valuable. Five others were examined, each one ornate.

"Well, your Asa Sidney was a collector," Ned remarked, "and I must say he had good taste. What are you going to do with these?"

Nancy did not know. "I suppose they shouldn't be moved, but I'm afraid to leave them. They may be stolen."

"Perhaps we can put back the grass cloth so the cuts won't be noticeable," Ned suggested.

The swords were replaced and the safe shut. Putting back the frail grass cloth was a tedious job. Nancy had noticed a jar of paste in the room Carol had occupied. She went to get it, then worked with Ned for some time. Finally Nancy felt that the repair would suffice until the authorities came to appraise the estate.

"Where do we look next?" Ned asked. "This is a lot more exciting than my job was as camp counselor."

"Please don't tell anyone what you found," Nancy cautioned.

"Why, Miss Drew," Ned said, "do you think you should address an 'officer' that way?"

The two burst into laughter, recalling Jacob Sidney's mistaken impression. Then they became serious.

"I think we've done enough for one visit," Nancy said. "But before we leave I want to go upstairs and see if the lock is intact on the door to the tower room."

She went up the steps, followed by Ned.

"This sure is a spooky old house," he remarked. "I wouldn't want to live in it."

"But great for a mystery," Nancy said. "Well, nobody has managed to remove this seal, but I'm sure it has been tampered with. I must—"

At that moment a frightful howl echoed through the old inn. Then came a reverberating crash!

CHAPTER XVI

The Ruse

THE crash and ear-piercing yell startled Nancy and Ned.

"What was that?" he asked. "It sounded right outside!"

They both went to the stairway window and struggled to lift the stiff, warped sash.

Nancy leaned out. "Oh!" she cried. "A man's on the porch roof with a ladder on top of him!"

Ned looked down. "It isn't the guard," he said. "Who can he be?"

"We'd better run down," Nancy suggested, "and help the poor man."

The couple raced down the steps to the second floor and made their way to a front room, whose windows opened onto the roof of the porch. The man lay unconscious beneath the ladder. Nancy and Ned climbed out to the roof and pulled the ladder off the prostrate form.

"I never saw him before," Nancy said. "Evidently he was trying to get into the house."

"I'll go down and get the guard," Ned offered.

In a few minutes he was back to report that the guard was not in sight.

"That's strange," said Nancy. "Anyway, I think this man should go to the hospital. Ned, will you drive to a phone and call the police to send an ambulance?"

"I hate to leave you alone here, Nancy."

"Oh, I'll be all right," she assured him.

Reluctantly Ned hurried to his car and drove off. Nancy decided to hunt for the guard.

As she neared the hall, she heard a step behind her and turned. The man whom she had thought to be unconscious stood there, an evil grin on his face! Nancy started to run, but he caught her in an iron grasp.

"Let go of me!" she demanded.

He gave a mean laugh. "I got my orders to get rid of you!" the man mumbled. Nancy now realized he had been faking unconsciousness all the time.

"Who gave you the orders? Frank Jemitt?"

"You know too much," the man answered.

As she struggled to get away, the man pulled a small bottle from his pocket and waved it under her nose. Nancy held her breath, all the while fighting like a tigress. She heard a car drive in. If she could only hold out until help came!

But the room began to reel. Nancy couldn't breathe. Then she blacked out. When the young sleuth revived, she was lying underneath a bed. Its deep-fringed spread hid her from view.

"I guess that's why no one found me," she thought. Her head ached. "I need fresh air."

Staggering, she made her way to the window. Vaguely she noticed that the ladder was still there.

"Where is everybody?" Nancy wondered. Suddenly she noticed that Ned's car was not in sight. "Hasn't he come back yet?"

A sudden fear gripped her. Had the powerful stranger knocked Ned out when he returned, hid him some place, and then taken his car?

Feeling stronger now, Nancy decided to investigate. Going from room to room, she called loudly for Ned, but received no answer. Panic-stricken, Nancy began to search under beds and in closets. Ned was nowhere in sight.

Sitting down on the steps of the front porch, Nancy tried to imagine what had happened during her blackout. "I must think," she told herself. "This is dreadful! What'll I do? No phone, no car—"

Her eyes were suddenly attracted to a startling sight. A pair of men's feet protruded from beneath the porch! Ned's? Sick with fear, Nancy jumped up, seized the man's ankles, and pulled him out.

"The guard! He's been drugged too!"

Almost at once the man's eyelids flickered open and presently he was able to tell Nancy what had happened. He had been knocked out by the same man who had drugged her.

"I shouldn't have trusted that guy."

Nancy told the guard that she was alarmed over the safety of the young man who had come there with her.

"I wish I could help you," the guard said.

Just then a car turned into the driveway and Nancy's heart leaped. It was Ned's! She rushed to meet him.

"Nancy! You're all right! Where did you go?"

"I was under a bed asleep."

"What!"

She told what had happened to her and the guard. Ned was astounded.

"I'm glad you're okay," he said, stepping from the car and putting an arm about her shoulders. "The police and I thought you'd been kidnapped. They're still looking for you."

"And I thought you had been knocked out also. What did happen?" Nancy asked.

Ned explained that soon after he had returned from making the phone call, the ambulance had arrived, only to find that the "patient" had vanished.

"I immediately called the Inlet Village police and they sent three men out here right away. You were well hidden, Nancy. When you didn't answer our calls, we figured that fellow kidnapped you.

"I had to go to headquarters and give a description of you along with his. The police are now combing the highway and turn-offs. Nancy, I came back here just in case—"

Before he could finish, a small truck pulled up in front of the inn. It belonged to the telephone company and in a short time their man had the service restored. At once Ned called police headquarters to brief the captain on the situation. He said efforts would be doubled to find the stranger.

"Tell Miss Drew we haven't picked up any information about the Jemitts," the captain said.

When Ned relayed the message, Nancy remarked, "I have a hunch the Jemitts sent that stranger who knocked me and the guard out. If we could find him, he might lead us to them."

"But not tonight." Ned was firm about Nancy returning home.

"On one condition," she answered. "That you stay to dinner."

"Agreed."

Nancy telephoned her father and suggested another guard be sent out to relieve the one who had been drugged.

"I'll attend to it at once, Nancy."

"There's a lot more to tell you, Dad, but let's wait until dinnertime. By the way, when will I be able to go into the tower room? I'm sure the answer to many secrets is right there."

"You may go in tomorrow afternoon," the lawyer replied. "Men from the courthouse and an appraiser will be there in the morning. The door to the tower is to be kept locked even after the appraisal is completed. But I'll give you my key."

"Great. Ned and I are coming home now. See you later."

Nancy explained to the guard that he would be relieved in a short time, adding, "Will you be all right if we go now?"

"Oh yes. I have a slight headache but otherwise I feel okay."

When Nancy and Ned were about halfway home, he looked at the gasoline gauge and said, "I couldn't make it to River Heights without filling up. Is there a station near here?"

"Yes," she replied. "Take the next road to the right to Maywood."

Ned drove there. As the tank was being filled, Nancy glanced at a car headed for Maywood. Her pulse quickened. The driver was the man who had drugged her and the guard!

"Hurry!" she called to the attendant. As Ned looked at her, puzzled, Nancy whispered, "I just saw the man who knocked me out. We must follow him!"

Ned called out to the attendant, "That'll be enough." The surprised man shut off the pump.

Ned glanced at the price gauge and quickly paid for the gasoline. "Keep the change," he said.

"Where'd the man go?" Ned asked Nancy.

"Toward Maywood. Oh, please hurry. He ought to be arrested, and besides, he may be going to meet the Jemitts."

The suspect was not driving fast and Ned soon caught up. "Now what do we do?" he asked.

"See where he goes and then get a policeman."

Presently the man turned into an old area of Maywood where the houses were in a shabby state. He parked in front of one on which hung a sign: *Mrs. Dilberry's Guest House.* The man let himself in with a key.

"Ned, go for the police, will you? I'll wait here in case he or the Jemitts come out."

"Promise me," he said, cupping Nancy's chin in his hand, "that you won't disappear again."

"Not even to chase them?"

"No." Ned sat still until she gave her word, then hurried off. Nancy got out and stood back of a tall hedge so she could not be seen from the windows of the guest house.

It was not long before Ned returned with two plainclothes detectives who he introduced as Manton and Wright. Manton said he would cover the rear door of the house while the others went inside.

A woman in her sixties answered their ring. Detective Wright showed his badge and asked if she was Mrs. Dilberry. When she replied Yes, he said, "You have a guest here who is wanted for assault."

"Not here," Mrs. Dilberry declared. "All my folks are respectable."

"If you don't cooperate," he said, "you will be liable for aiding and abetting a criminal. He just came in here. Where is he?"

"You mean Mr. Krill?" A look of fright had come over Mrs. Dilberry's face. "He's in the room at the head of the stairs."

As Wright and Ned started up the stairway, Nancy paused to ask the woman a question. "Do you have any guests here named Jemitt?"

"I did have but they moved out about an hour ago," Mrs. Dilberry said. "Right after the husband got a phone call."

"Where did they go?" Nancy asked.

"They didn't say, miss."

"Tell me," Nancy went on, "were they friendly with Mr. Krill?"

"Oh my, yes! I could hear them walking back and forth to each other's rooms all the time."

"Thank you," Nancy said, then dashed up the steps to confront the suspect.

CHAPTER XVII

A Capture

AT first Krill refused to open the door. But when Wright said he had witnesses to identify him as the person who had been at The Sign of the Twisted Candles that afternoon, and there was no sense in breaking down the door, the suspect unlocked it.

"You got nothin' on me," he declared.

Nancy stepped forward. "I accuse you of drugging me and the guard, and of being in league with the Jemitts to steal from the Sidney mansion."

Krill's jaw dropped. "H-how did you know that? I was a nut to tie up with them."

The detective said, "You'd better tell us all you know."

"I ain't sayin' another word!" Krill shouted.

"Okay, come along. Miss Drew, will you tell Manton to meet us at the car?"

Nancy went downstairs ahead of the men and relayed the message. Manton joined the others at the curb.

"Please follow us," Wright requested Nancy and Ned. "Miss Drew, you will have to prefer charges against this man downtown."

They drove to police headquarters. Nancy signed the necessary papers and Krill was taken to a cell. Finally she and Ned set off for River Heights.

Ned suddenly burst into laughter. "One thing that makes you so interesting, Nancy, is that I never know when I ask you to go out, what mystery will come our way!"

Nancy chuckled. "And I never know myself. Now if I could only get hold of the Jemitts that easily—"

"I'm betting on you," Ned replied. Then, putting a hand over hers, he added, "But please be careful. They're dangerous."

It was late by the time the couple reached Nancy's house. Mr. Drew was already there and declared he was "hungry as a bear," but wanted full details on his daughter's afternoon activities.

"First we're going to eat," Hannah Gruen declared, "or the roast beef will be ruined. And no harrowing tales until the dinner is over. We want our guests to enjoy their dinner."

Mr. Drew shrugged and smiled, but obeyed the instructions. Nancy said, "Carol, I can't wait to

see your Butterfly Pie." When it was served, everyone gave gasps of delight and Nancy exclaimed,
"Why, Carol, it's a work of art!"

Into each portion of the lemon chiffon pie
Carol had stuck two large wafers which she had
fashioned into the shape of butterfly wings. Carol
had decorated them in various patterns with
vegetable colorings.

"Nancy's right," said Mr. Drew, "and the pie
tastes even better than it looks." Carol blushed
and smiled appreciatively.

After dinner the Drews and their friends gathered in the living room, and the full story was told
with special emphasis on the finding of the antique swords and the arrest of Krill. In order not
to alarm Carol, Nancy's encounter with Krill was
dealt with lightly.

But Carol was serious. "It's marvelous what
you're all doing for me, but you mustn't take such
risks. *Please.*"

Presently Ned stood up and said he must leave.
"I have to get up early tomorrow and drive to
Emerson. Football practice starts early this year."

After he had left, Nancy asked her father at
what time the next day she might visit the Sidney
mansion. The lawyer replied, "I'll be leaving at
seven in the morning to open the house for the
men who will be appraising it. Why don't you
and Carol have a leisurely breakfast and then

drive out? When we've finished our inventory, you can do some more treasure hunting."

Nancy's eyes twinkled. "Oh, that would be great, Dad! I'll ask Carol. She's out in the kitchen helping Hannah."

When Carol heard the request, her lower lip began to tremble. "Oh, do I have to go?" she said, tears coming to her eyes. "I—I— Nancy, that place haunts me. At first, I didn't seem to mind so much. But now it's so pleasant here, and the inn is so full of horrible memories. When Mr. Sidney went, every bit of happiness left that old house."

Nancy put an arm about the girl. "I'm sure I'd feel the same way, Carol, and Dad will certainly understand."

She returned to her father, who agreed to Carol's request.

Nancy said to him, "What do you think of my asking Bess and George? After all, they are beneficiaries."

Her father smiled. "Do you think the feud has calmed down enough?"

"I'm willing to take the chance," Nancy replied.

She went to the telephone and asked Bess. "Oh!" her friend exclaimed, evidently shocked by the proposal.

Nancy went on, "After all the *known* possessions of Mr. Asa Sidney are listed, and the valuable ones removed to the bank, Dad said I might hunt for further hidden treasures. It would be fun to have you there and, after all, it was Mr. Sidney's request that you and George help hunt. You might find something yourself! What do you say?"

"You've persuaded me," said Bess, "but I'll have to ask my parents."

Bess was gone from the telephone so long Nancy concluded the answer would be No, or there would be some counterproposal. She was relieved when the answer was, "It's okay. And my parents said to tell you they're glad we've made up."

"I'll stop for you at nine-thirty," Nancy said. "Dad is driving out earlier."

Then she called George. Mr. and Mrs. Fayne had to be consulted but willingly gave their permission. George said, "I hope we find a million dollars!"

On the way to the mansion the next day, Nancy brought the cousins up to date on what had happened since she had last seen them.

"Nancy, how ghastly!" Bess exclaimed.

George scowled. "I hope I'm around if that man Jemitt shows up. I'd like to help capture him."

When the girls arrived at the inn, Mr. Drew was busy with two men. They were Mr. Harris, a representative of the government, and Mr.

Thompson, an appraiser. As soon as they had made an inventory of the furnishings, Mr. Drew asked Nancy to show them the swords, the music box, and the diamond bracelet. Then just before the three men left with these treasures, Mr. Drew gave Nancy the key to the tower room.

By this time it was one o'clock. Bess announced she was hungry. When and where were they going to eat?

"Right here," Nancy replied. "Carol packed a lunch for us. I'll get it out of the car."

While they were enjoying roast beef sandwiches, Nancy told her friends that the Fernwood Orphanage was planning to find new foster parents for Carol.

"She's darling," said Bess. "I wouldn't mind having her live with us."

As the last of the lunch was finished, George said, "Where do we start our search?"

"Let's go to the tower first," Nancy suggested.

They mounted the stairs, and Nancy unlocked the door. The tower room seemed stuffy, so she opened the big front window, then locked the entrance door.

Bess, gazing around, said, "What is it about this room that seems so different from the night we were here?"

"The twisted candles," Nancy replied. "They're not lighted."

George agreed. "Some of them are standing in such odd places. I wonder if that's significant of anything."

The three girls began picking them up one by one. Nancy chose two handsome, stately twisted candles in silver holders which stood on one end of the brick fireplace.

"I believe these pieces," she said, "are covering something valuable."

Nancy placed a rush-bottomed chair before the yawning opening of the fireplace, and stepped up. Carefully she moved the heavy candles away, then ran her fingers over the shelf.

Was she imagining it or had a brick moved? At once Nancy set to work prying out the loose brick. It was a tedious job but presently she lifted out the brick. Beneath lay a tightly rolled brown suede bag bound with a leather thong.

"Girls, look!" she exclaimed.

She quickly stepped off the chair and laid the bag on it.

"What can it be?" Bess asked.

"I don't know, but it's heavy," Nancy answered as she untied the fastening and spread out the long, narrow bag.

Revealed were tiny pockets containing a collection of old coins!

"Oh!" George cried. "They're probably worth a mint!"

For safekeeping Nancy replaced the bag, the

"Here's a secret compartment!" Nancy cried out

brick, and the candles. Then she went to examine the opposite end of the shelf. It contained a similar bag but this one held jewelry.

"I can't believe it!" Bess exclaimed. "Nancy, you've earned part of this treasure."

The young detective waved aside the suggestion and said, "I'm hoping to find a secret that's more valuable than old coins or jewelry."

Nancy walked slowly toward the massive, carved desk-table next to the front window. On it was the biggest twisted candle of all. The towering object stood next to a well-worn old leather Bible that Nancy reverently moved to one side. Within the exposed, dust-free area she detected hairline cracks that marked an oblong about a foot wide and fourteen inches in length.

"Here's a secret compartment!" she cried out, and her friends rushed to her side.

Nancy's fingers searched for a spring which might release the lid. At length they found a slight indentation on the underside of the kneehole.

She pushed it and the top of the secret compartment flew open, revealing a recess about six inches deep. Nancy peered inside at an orderly pile of letters. The top envelope said, *For Carol Wipple. To be opened* . . . Nancy tried to remain calm about her startling discovery.

"I think I'd better not disturb these," she told her friends, firmly shutting the lid and pushing the Bible back over it. She wanted to discuss the discovery with her father before revealing what she had seen.

Before the girls could continue the search, there was a loud pounding on the door.

"Who is it?" Nancy asked.

"The guard. Miss Drew, there's a phone call for you. The woman on the other end of the line is frantic."

Nancy unlocked the door and the girls hurried out. She relocked it, and dashed down the stairs.

Hannah Gruen was calling. "Oh, Nancy, my news is terrible!" she exclaimed. "Carol has been kidnapped!"

CHAPTER XVIII

Valuable Clue

"KIDNAPPED!" Nancy fairly shrieked. "Oh no! When? How?"

"I don't know." Hannah Gruen's voice was shaky. "Please come right home. I phoned your father's office, but Miss Hanson said he's in court and can't be disturbed."

"I'll come as fast as I can get there," Nancy promised.

When she relayed the message to Bess and George, they were horrified and dashed out to the car with her. All the way to the Drew home Bess kept murmuring, "Poor Carol," and George said, "I'm sure those awful Jemitts did it and will hold her for ransom."

Nancy remained silent. Conflicting ideas raced through her mind. She tried to convince herself that Carol had left of her own accord and would either telephone or return soon.

When Nancy reached the house, this bright thought was dashed. Hannah Gruen was pacing the floor.

"I went to the store for a short time and left Carol here," the housekeeper explained. "She promised to keep the doors and windows locked and to let no one in. Oh, what shall we do?"

George suggested notifying the police, but Nancy said, "Let's wait until my father comes. He should be home soon. Hannah, why are you so sure Carol was kidnapped?"

"Because the laundryman came here right after I got home. When I told him what I suspected, he said he'd seen a car pull out of our driveway with a young girl in it just as he arrived."

"Who was with her?"

"A couple. From the man's description, I suppose it was the Jemitts. Where do you think they took her?"

"I wish I knew," Nancy replied, terribly worried herself.

She decided to take George's advice and call Police Chief McGinnis. He was alarmed at the turn of events.

"So far no police have found any trace of the Jemitts," he said. "It's possible they're in hiding somewhere. In any case, if there's no word by tomorrow, I'll notify the FBI. In the meantime there may be a ransom note. Nancy, I think I should warn you about getting into the same predicament yourself. After all, the Jemitts no doubt consider you their most formidable enemy."

"One thing puzzles me," Nancy said. "The Jemitts were remembered in the will. Why are they acting like this?"

"Probably to coerce your friend into signing a paper promising them a large portion of her inheritance for taking care of her. They may even get her signature on a letter begging the Fernwood Orphanage to let the Jemitts remain as her foster parents."

"She'll never do it," Nancy told the chief.

"Under a threat she may."

Nancy was not convinced, but Hannah, Bess, and George were. The cousins felt that their parents should know what had happened and telephoned them. The Faynes and Marvins promised to help all they could and then came to pick up their daughters.

Mr. Drew arrived soon afterward and was as disturbed as the others by the kidnapping. He notified the orphanage of Carol's disappearance and of their suspicions. None of them ate much dinner, each lost in thought.

Finally Nancy said, "Dad, what are visiting hours at the jails?"

"They're not all the same, dear. Why?"

"I'd like to talk to Krill. Maybe I can get him to reveal where the Jemitts are hiding."

"Not a bad idea," the lawyer said. "If nothing

breaks by tomorrow morning, I'll go with you to Maywood."

Although no telephone messages or callers came during the night, Hannah and the Drews slept poorly and they were up early. Mr. Drew telephoned the jail and found that in his case an exception would be made to the rule of afternoon visitors only. He and his daughter could come at ten.

As Nancy was about to go for her car, the telephone rang and she rushed to answer it. An unfamiliar voice, speaking with a foreign accent, said, "Is this Nancy Drew?"

"Yes."

"I call to warn you not try find Carol Wipple or both of you be harmed." The stranger hung up.

Hannah had been standing close enough to hear the message. She turned to Mr. Drew. "Please don't let Nancy out of your sight. Someone has just threatened her!"

"I shan't," he said.

The Drews rode quickly to the Maywood jail and were taken to Krill's cell.

The prisoner was defiant. "I said I ain't talkin'," he greeted them.

"To the police perhaps, but how about just to us?" Mr. Drew suggested.

"Huh! And have you blab it to them? No, sir." Krill turned his back on the callers.

Nancy was convinced this man could not be

wheedled into giving information about the Jemitts. She used another method.

"Mr. Krill, there's been a kidnapping and you're involved," she said.

The prisoner did an about-face and yelled, "I am not! I told Frank I wouldn't have any part of it!" Suddenly he stared at Nancy "Who was kidnapped? You were supposed to be the one!"

Mr. Drew spoke up. "Things will go a lot easier with you, Krill, if you tell everything you know."

The prisoner walked up and down nervously. "I needed money. Frank Jemitt said he knew an easy way to get it and that would square him with me. I'd done him a big favor. In return he'd pay me well to get Nancy Drew off the case and try to find some papers hidden in the tower room by the man who died.

"He told me where the ladder was. When you drove in, Miss Drew, I thought up the scheme to fool and drug you. But I couldn't take you along with me because your boy friend was around. I knew Jemitt would be mad because he told me to bring you to—"

"Yes?" Nancy said.

Krill walked back and forth several times before replying. At last he said, "I may as well tell you. The Jemitts own a little cottage along a branch of the Muskoka River. I don't know exactly where it is, but they said it was sort of in a

woods at the end of a road called something like
'student.' They call the cottage Restview, I think."

Just then a guard came to say, "Time's up, Mr.
Drew."

Nancy was thrilled by what they had learned.
"Dad, can you go there with me right away?" she
asked as soon as they were outside.

"I wouldn't miss the chance." He smiled.

Looking for a road with a name like "student"
that ran to a branch of the Muskoka proved to be
frustrating. After two hours of fruitless searching
Nancy and her father stopped for lunch at a road-
side restaurant. They discussed where to go next.

Presently they became aware of a woman at the
next table who seemed to be interested in their
conversation. Finally she leaned over and said,
"Perhaps I can be of some help. Do you think the
road you're looking for could be Steuben? There
is such a road about a mile from here. It leads
directly to the water."

"Oh, thank you," said Nancy. "We'll try it."

To the Drews' delight, Steuben Road led directly to Restview Cottage. There were no other
houses around. No car was in sight and the place
appeared to be deserted.

"I guess the Jemitts aren't using this," Mr.
Drew remarked.

"But they may have left Carol here," Nancy
said. "We must find out."

She and her father stepped from their car and knocked on the door. There was no answer and not a sound inside or outside the cottage.

"Carol may be tied and gagged," Nancy said. "We *must* make sure she isn't in there."

"I agree." Mr. Drew was grim.

They walked around the building and began looking in the windows. No one was in sight. Suddenly Nancy grabbed her father's arm and pointed into the living room.

"See those boxes along the wall? They're just like the ones Frank Jemitt was taking out of the tenant house at Asa Sidney's. And they're marked like the cartons I saw in the warehouse yard. I'm sure they contain stolen property!"

"You're probably right," the lawyer agreed. "We have no right to break in, of course. I guess we'd better—"

He stopped speaking as they heard a car coming. Nancy and her father braced themselves. Were they going to come face to face with the Jemitts and perhaps Carol?

In a few seconds they saw the approaching sedan was not that of the Jemitts, but a police car. The driver was a state trooper, who said he was on a routine checkup of all roads in the vicinity.

"You're just the man we need," Mr. Drew told him and showed his business card. "This is my daughter Nancy."

"I've heard of you both," the trooper said. "My name's Hatch. What can I do for you?"

"Tell him, Nancy."

After hearing the story, Trooper Hatch said, "We mustn't lose any time. I'll force a window and we'll go in."

The three climbed into the living room. First they looked for Carol and called her name several times. She was not there. Nancy was disappointed. Now the search would have to be continued. But where?

"Let's examine these boxes," Mr. Drew suggested.

Nancy and the two men began to untie them. She had chosen a heavy cardboard box with many perforations in the top. Nancy knelt on one knee, pulled off the lid, then shrieked in terror!

CHAPTER XIX

A Risky Climb

THE box contained a large copper-colored snake! Disturbed, it reared and the head darted toward Nancy, fangs out.

In horror she fell backward and scrambled out of the way. The snake wriggled to the floor. By this time Mr. Drew and the trooper had picked up iron fireplace tools and quickly killed the reptile.

"Oh, thank you," said Nancy. As Trooper Hatch dragged the snake outside, Nancy recovered from her fright and went to look in its box. A velvet cloth was spread across the bottom of it. Nancy whipped it off, wondering if she would find more snakes beneath. Instead, she saw a large quantity of flat silverware on which the initial S was engraved.

"Asa Sidney's silver!" Nancy exclaimed, and told the trooper about the thefts and her father's responsibility for the silver as executor of the estate.

Trooper Hatch nodded understandingly. "We'll look for anything else marked S, and whatever other objects you recognize, we'll take to headquarters."

More flatware and an initialed silver coffee service were found, but nothing else that could be definitely identified as Asa Sidney's property.

"Do you think," Nancy asked the trooper, "that the Jemitts will come here?"

"If they're sure nobody knows about the place, I believe they will." He grinned. "I'll have this property staked out."

Nancy and her father led the way from Steuben Road. "Do you suppose," she asked him, "that Carol knew about Restview Cottage but didn't mention it?"

"I doubt that she ever heard about it or she would have told you," the lawyer replied. "The Jemitts may have used the place as a temporary drop for their stolen goods."

Despite the progress that had been made in solving the mystery of the thefts, Nancy reflected sadly that Carol had not been found. "There's not one single clue," she said to herself.

When they reached River Heights, Nancy told her father she would like to stop at his office and make a few telephone calls. First she got in touch with Hannah, who had no news to report. Next, Nancy called the Fernwood Orphanage but they had heard nothing.

Then she tried Police Chief McGinnis. There was still no clue to Carol, or her foster parents' whereabouts, he told her.

Nancy said, "I have one good thing to tell you, Chief." She gave a detailed account of the trips to Maywood and Restview Cottage.

Chief McGinnis chuckled. "You're certainly on the job, Nancy."

After she hung up the phone, Nancy asked her father for his report from the two guards. Both had called in to say no one had come to the tenant house and the only visitor to the inn had been Jacob Sidney. "He was not admitted."

"I wonder what he wanted," Nancy said to her father, then added quickly, "Guess Ned's warning wasn't enough to keep Jacob from the Sidney mansion."

That evening Mr. Hill came to dinner. Directly afterward, Nancy said to him and her father, "I have a new idea where the Jemitts may be hiding Carol."

"Where?"

"At The Sign of the Twisted Candles."

The men were amazed at this deduction. "But with a guard there constantly, how could three of them get in without being seen?" Mr. Hill objected.

"Mr. Jemitt is clever," Nancy answered. "He probably used a key to one of the doors while the guard was patrolling the other side of the house.

Dad, won't you and Mr. Hill go out there with me?"

Mr. Drew smiled. "Everything else has failed. I suppose we may as well try this."

The three set off with dire warnings from Hannah Gruen. As they reached the driveway leading to the inn, Nancy suggested that she and her companions walk the rest of the way and go cautiously.

"Good idea," her father agreed.

He locked the car and they set off on foot. Not a word was spoken. The three walked as noiselessly as possible, but were puzzled as to why the watchman did not come to see who was approaching.

Nancy thought, "If the Jemitts *are* here, maybe they knocked him out!"

The Drews and Mr. Hill circled the house, but did not see the watchman. "I don't like this," Nancy's father said. "But let's walk around once more."

As the two men started off, Nancy did not follow. She was contemplating the front of the building. Her eyes swept up and down the sprawling contours, then stopped at the window of the tower room.

"Is that a light?" she suddenly asked herself.

The window seemed to show a lesser degree of darkness than the blank panes elsewhere in the house. Nancy looked more sharply.

"I believe the window has been covered so a

light won't shine through," she said to herself. "That certainly looks like a crack of light at the bottom."

Nancy started for the front door but realized that her father had the key. She could not afford to lose a moment in investigating the tower room. But how would she get in?

Suddenly the young detective remembered the ladder on the porch roof, where Krill had played his trick on her. Perhaps it was still there!

Flanking the porch steps on either side were stout lattices. Nancy reached through the vines and gripped the sturdy wooden support. Her toes found a foothold, and she was soon stepping over the edge of the porch roof.

Yes, there was the ladder! It was slow work to handle the ladder without making a sound, but Nancy managed to rest the top rung just below the sill of the tower window.

She carefully mounted the rungs. The ladder gave a sickening lurch as she came close to the top. Nancy reached up and clung to the sill.

She did not dare look downward for fear of losing her balance. With most of her weight supported by her hands Nancy continued her climb. Two steps more, and she was able to put her forearm on the sill and curl her fingers around the iron peg that once had held shutters. Cautiously Nancy raised her head until both eyes were on a level with the window frame.

Nancy could hear the low rumble of a masculine voice! Frank Jemitt's!

Taking infinite pains to retain her balance, she thrust her fingers under the edge of the window. Nancy was rewarded as the sash moved upward half an inch, an inch, and yet another half inch. Then the frame gave a tiny squeak and seemed to stick. For one breathless moment Nancy ducked her head and waited to see if anyone came to the window to investigate.

To her relief, the voice droned on without interruption. Nancy again dared to raise her eyes to the level of the sill. The cloth had evidently been fastened to the inner frame, not to the sash, because the gap she had made by raising the window was still covered.

Although Nancy could not see inside the tower room, she could hear plainly what Frank Jemitt was saying:

"—you and that Drew girl spent a lot of time up here. I'm sure you know where the papers I want are hidden. Don't sniffle. Where are they?"

No answer.

Jemitt went on, "And there are hidden treasures in this room. If you'll tell us where the stuff is, you'll get your share. If you don't, then you got to be hurt until you do."

"I've told you I don't know," a weepy-voiced girl answered. *Carol!*

The relief Nancy felt at having located her

friend was instantly dispelled by Jemitt's next threat.

"I'll give you one minute more to tell, and then you'll get a taste of this whip!"

Mrs. Jemitt added her own threat. "What's more, if you won't tell us, we'll get Nancy Drew as easy as we got you. We'll set a trap for her because we'll make you phone her to come to see you secretly. Then you can watch us force *her* to tell!"

"Oh, please don't," Carol begged. "I'll do anything for you, but don't harm Nancy."

"Time's up!" Mrs. Jemitt said.

Nancy, shaken with horror, lifted the cloth that hung over the window. She peered in on a strange drama.

Carol, her new dress rumpled and her hair in disarray, stood leaning against the old desk-table with the secret drawer, not three feet from Nancy. Her face was turned in profile as she stared at Frank Jemitt. His wife stood with arms folded, an evil smile on her face, while he slowly rolled up his sleeves. Then he picked up a thick willow reed.

"Open the closet, Emma," he said. "We'll stick this girl in there when we're through with her."

Mrs. Jemitt turned toward a door in the wall.

Nancy had less than a minute to act! While the attention of the couple was momentarily diverted, she reached through the opening and tapped on the desk.

"Carol!" she whispered.

At the voice coming out of nowhere Carol's overwrought nerves snapped. She screamed loudly and toppled to the floor.

"What's going on?" Jemitt cried.

He wheeled and saw the fluttering cloth at the window. With a snarl he rushed forward, his hands thrust out. Nancy was sure he meant to topple the ladder on which she swayed.

CHAPTER XX

Startling Confession

At that moment a muffled scream reached the ears of Nancy's father and Mr. Hill.

"What was that? It came from upstairs in the house!" Mr. Drew exclaimed. "Quick! Inside!"

He unlocked the front door and the two men rushed in. Snapping on lights as they went, the two ran to the second floor.

"No one here," said Mr. Drew. He led the way to the tower room, two steps at a time. The door to it was closed but not locked. An intruder had evidently opened it! Mr. Drew burst in, followed by the banker.

An amazing and uncanny scene met their gaze. Nancy Drew's head and shoulders were framed in the window as if she were standing on air. Frank Jemitt's arms were thrust through the opening, in the act of pushing Nancy backward. The young detective's hands were clutching the man's wrists to prevent her from falling.

Carol's arms were clasped around Jemitt's waist, straining to pull him away from Nancy. And Mrs. Jemitt was just in the act of bringing down the heavy willow reed across Carol's shoulders!

"Stop!" thundered Carson Drew, leaping forward.

With one sweep of his arm he sent Mrs. Jemitt reeling aside. Raymond Hill grabbed her husband, while Mr. Drew reached out the window to rescue Nancy. He was not a moment too soon, for the ladder on which she was standing slipped from under her and crashed to the ground.

Mr. Drew helped Nancy through the window, while Carol guarded the door toward which her foster mother had dashed.

"Let me go!" Jemitt croaked. He was being half choked by Mr. Hill's grasp.

The banker released his prisoner, who staggered into a corner, clutching at his throat.

"Nancy, are you all right?" her father asked.

"Yes, Dad, but you came just in the nick of time."

"Oh, Nancy," Carol cried out, "you were almost hurt because of me! It was my scream that gave you away."

"But it was what warned us," Mr. Drew told

her. "Raymond, please go down to the phone booth and call State Police headquarters. Ask them to send troopers to take charge of two prisoners."

As Mr. Hill went off, Nancy turned to Jemitt. "Where's the watchman?"

"See if you can find out," was the surly reply.

"I can answer that," Carol spoke up. "My foster father punched him. While the man was kind of groggy, Mr. Jemitt tied his arms and legs and gagged him. He's in the big closet under the stairs on the first floor."

"I'll get him," Nancy volunteered. "Come on, Carol."

The guard, shamefaced at having been trapped a second time, eagerly took charge of the two prisoners. While waiting for the State Police car to arrive, the Jemitts made a full confession. Many of Nancy's hunches had been correct. Jemitt also said he had put the snake in the box to frighten off any burglars.

By this time the police had arrived and the Jemitts were in custody.

After they had gone, Mr. Hill asked, "Now what do we do? Shall we call it a night?"

Nancy answered quickly, "No, let's not. I want to phone all the beneficiaries of Asa Sidney's estate and ask them to come here at once."

The others turned questioning eyes toward Nancy. She went on, "During my search in the tower room I came across a hidden letter from Mr. Sidney marked 'For Carol Wipple. To be opened in the presence of Peter Boonton, Jacob Sidney, Anna and Bess Marvin, and Louise and George Fayne.' I think it will explain why he left most of his money to you, Carol."

"Oh!" the girl exclaimed.

"Do you mind if they come?" Nancy asked.

Carol sighed. "We may as well get it over with."

Nancy went to the telephone. In turn each one she called was glad to hear that Carol had been found and was shocked to learn of the Jemitts' cruelty. The relatives demurred, however, about coming to the inn at that late hour, but finally consented.

"Carol, when did you last eat?" Nancy asked when she rejoined the others.

"Not for a long time. I lost my appetite."

"Then let's have a bite before the Sidneys and Boontons begin to arrive."

Carol managed a smile. "I guess I'll need some strength. Nancy, I let the Jemitts into your house and they threatened me, and made me come here. How can you ever forgive me?"

Nancy smiled. "You're already forgiven. Now let's look for some food."

The kitchen cupboards had little in them but Nancy found canned chocolate milk, potted ham, and some relatively fresh bread. She made a sandwich and heated the milk. Carol had just finished eating when the Marvins arrived. Within a few minutes all the relatives had assembled.

"Miss Drew, your reason for getting me out here this late," said Jacob Sidney, "had better be good."

"I'm sure it will be," Nancy replied. "Will you all please come up to the tower room."

Carol grabbed Nancy's hand as they ascended the steps. She was trembling.

"Don't be afraid," Nancy whispered. "I have a hunch there's a wonderful surprise for you in the letter."

Mr. Drew unlocked the door to the tower room and the many candles were lighted. When everyone was seated, the lawyer briefly outlined what had happened since they had last been together, told of the recovered treasures, and the Jemitts' part in stealing some of Asa Sidney's property.

"And now Nancy will show you where she found the letter to Carol," he concluded.

A great hush came over the room as his daughter walked to the desk-table. She pushed the big Bible aside and pressed the secret spring. As the lid of the hidden compartment flew up, the onlookers gasped.

"There are many papers in here," Nancy said, "but the letter on top is the one to be read now."

She gave it to Carol, but the overwrought girl's hand shook so hard she dropped the envelope.

"Nancy, please read it for me," she begged.

There was a pause as Nancy picked up the letter. Again she gave Carol a chance to read it, but the other girl only shook her head. *"Please."*

"All right." Nancy opened the letter and began to read.

" 'My dear Carol,

" 'This letter is the confession of a stubborn, selfish old man. For many years I have known the secret of your identity, but have not revealed it for two reasons: the feud in my family and the fact that I wanted to keep you near me. I have no direct descendants, but you are my great-grandniece.' "

At that revelation there were exclamations of surprise in the room and whisperings among the Boontons and Sidneys. Carol kept her head down, eyes closed. Her face was pale, and she sat perfectly still.

Mr. Drew said, "Go on, Nancy."

" 'There were only two people who ignored the senseless feud and for this reason were ostracized from their families. They were John Boonton, brother of Anna Marvin and Louise Fayne, and Helen Sidney, daughter of Jacob Sidney. When their families would not let them marry, they eloped, and later had a baby whom they named Carol after my little girl who died. That baby is you, Carol, my dear!' "

Suddenly Bess Marvin rushed to Carol. "You're my cousin!" she exclaimed, hugging the speechless girl.

George ran forward. "And you're a Boonton! You're Carol Boonton!"

Tears of joy streamed down Carol's cheeks. She smiled through them and looked at Nancy. "Oh, Nancy, if it hadn't been for you, I might never have known this!"

Nancy hugged her new friend while Mrs. Marvin said, "I shall ask the Fernwood Orphanage to appoint us as foster parents."

Mrs. Fayne said, "I want to share in this."

Mr. Drew had risen and asked for silence. "There is more to the letter. Nancy, please finish it."

Everyone sat down again and she went on.

" 'You will wonder how I learned all this. I was a director of the Fernwood Orphanage at the time you were brought there, Carol, by the rector of a nearby church. You were about two years old. He had found you near the altar, crying. A search for your parents proved hopeless.

" 'You were such a dear little thing and reminded me so much of my own little girl I asked that the orphanage change the name they had given you to Carol. The whole thing haunted me and I began some private detective work. I found out that a little while prior to the rector finding you, there had been an automobile accident not far away. The couple in it were killed. They proved to be Mr. and Mrs. John Boonton.

" 'A further search by me revealed that they were relatives of my wife, and among some papers they had left at a boarding house was a picture of you, Carol. Just as I was wondering what to do about revealing this secret, the Jemitts offered to become your foster parents. At a Board of Directors' meeting I said I would give my consent only if the Jemitts came to work here.

" 'You know the rest, Carol, and forgive me for being so selfish. I hope the fortune I am leaving you will more than offset any pain and privation I have caused you. I love you very much, Carol.

Asa Sidney' "

When Nancy stopped, all of Carol's relatives hurried to her side. Jacob Sidney put an arm around his new-found relative. "So I'm your grandfather, eh? Well, I must say that makes me very proud. Carol, please, don't hold what I've said against me, and I don't want one penny of your inheritance."

"Nor I," added Peter Boonton. He managed an apologetic grin. "After all I'm your great-uncle!"

Carol found it hard to say anything, but finally she whispered, "I can't believe it. Suddenly I have a grandfather, a great-uncle, two lovely aunts, and two wonderful cousins. And—and a most marvelous friend."

Her eyes searched the room for Nancy, who had

disappeared. Mr. Drew had left too. But in a few minutes both came back, saying they had been on the telephone.

"My dad has an announcement to make," she said, her eyes dancing.

The lawyer addressed the group. "We called the Fernwood Orphanage. Fortunately the Board of Directors was having a late-evening meeting. They agreed that since relatives of Carol's have been found who want her to make her home with them, the orphanage will waive any further claim."

A friendly argument between the Marvins and the Faynes followed. Both families wanted Carol to live with them. During the discussion, Nancy was wondering what her next mystery would be. It was a puzzling one, which was called *Password to Larkspur Lane.*

"We've decided, Nancy," Bess announced, "that Carol's going to spend most of her time at boarding school, and divide the rest between the Marvins and the Faynes."

"And I recommend that Carol learn judo," George said with a grin, "so if those horrible Jemitts should ever break jail, she'll know how to handle them!"

Everyone laughed and a thrill went through Nancy. The Boonton-Sidney feud was over!